THE MILE HIGH CLUB

THE MILE HIGH CLUB

PLANE SEX STORIES

EDITED BY

RACHEL KRAMER BUSSEL

Published in the United States by Cleis Press Inc., P.O. Box 14697, San Francisco, California 94114.

Printed in the United States.
Cover photogrpah: Patrik Giardino/CORBIS
Cover design: Scott Idleman
Text design: Frank Wiedemann
Cleis Press logo art: Juana Alicia
First Edition.
10 9 8 7 6 5 4 3 2 1

"34B" by Bill Kte'pi was originally published at Cleansheets.com under the byline Simon Caraway.

Contents

INTRODUCTION: FLYING HIGH

The Mile High Club is, for many, the stuff of legend, but I'm here to tell you that where there's a will, there's a way. Flying can bring out so many of our insecurities, fears, and frustrations, that it's natural we'd want to find a way to relieve all that tension by getting it on. Indeed, several of the stories here deal with sex as a way to conquer a fear of flying.

Just as I was completing this volume, I got a call from a friend who told me that on the way back from a family vacation, he got it on with a woman he ran into on the plane whom he'd known, but never slept with. They managed to have full-on intercourse (and much more) as the rest of the passengers slept—or so they thought! They found out later that they'd been true exhibitionists, seen by horny voyeurs.

In these stories, characters are often surprised to find themselves engaging in such risqué behavior midflight. The surprise and naughtiness make what's happening even hotter. For others, it's been carefully orchestrated, such as the woman meeting her online pen pal in "34B" or the one putting her arsenal of sex toys to good use in "Obedient."

Other scenarios are more fanciful, and, unless you're really lucky, are probably not going to happen to you. Part of the thrill of even thinking about the Mile High Club is that, in such close quarters, someone's bound to notice the movements, noises, and sensations of sex happening near him or her. Voyeurism and exhibitionism are part and parcel of sex on a plane, even if you never officially get caught.

I'm sure you are probably picturing getting it on in a tiny airplane bathroom, and yes, that happens here. But there's more than one way to join the Mile High Club, as the "Wild Child" in the story by Matt Conklin learns when her kinky new friend asks for some extra ice. And in "Bermuda Triangle," we're introduced to a threesome that takes edge play to new heights, as a man is blindfolded and instructed to fly, his fear upping the ante for the novel sexual encounter about to take place.

While this isn't a how-to manual, I'm sure you can pick up a few tips on the fine art of blanket placement and in-flight discretion from these talented writers. Alas, during the numerous flights I've taken in the last year, nothing so risqué has happened to me, but that hasn't stopped me from fantasizing about what might be going on a few rows over, or wondering, as I stand in the security line, who might try to pick me up. I love that Wi-Fi is the wave of the flying future, as I write about in my story "Urgent Message," and I'm looking forward to much in-the-air flirting.

Whether you're a member of the Mile High Club or just want to be, I hope these stories take you on some exciting trips, and that your next plane ride is just as eventful! Please feel free to share your story or keep up with what's new in plane sex at my blog at http://milehighclubbook.wordpress.com.

Rachel Kramer Bussel
New York City

34B

Bill Kte'pi

SWF seeks adventure. 34, attractive, strong, professional, healthy, happy. Seeking that missing piece and a man to take control. Tell me what you have to offer.

Every time the car hit one of those speed bumps on Airline Highway, you think about turning around. This is thrilling, yes—but stupid, too. Stupid to spend this kind of money over a man you've never met.

> *Nancy—be on the flight from Baltimore to Portland: I've pasted the itinerary at the bottom of this email. Buy a ticket for seat 34B. I'll reserve 34C. I'm buying two tickets; I'll leave C empty until it's time.*

Waiting in line for your ticket, waiting to board, you look at the men around you, even though you know he isn't one of them.

He'll board the second flight, when you switch planes in Baltimore. You don't know where he's from. He doesn't know where you're from.

As you go through security, you half hope you're stopped for something, that the emery board in your purse disqualifies you from air travel, that overzealous air marshals decide you're a threat to national security—and you get sent home to your matching plates and new stereo and warm safe bed.

You fidget on the plane to Baltimore, unable to concentrate on the paperback you brought in your purse. You glance down at your lap to see if anyone can tell you're not wearing panties. Baltimore is a forty-seven-minute layover that seems to stretch on for hours.

You board the second plane.

34B—it sounds like a bra size. You don't even know his name. You gave yours—your real name, though he may assume otherwise—but he never offered his and you didn't want to ask and have him say no. You didn't want to establish his right to tell you no that quickly.

This is stupid. But it's safe, isn't it?

He pointed that out when you hinted at your uncertainty a month ago: *It's an airplane. What is it you think I can do without you letting me do it?*

34C is empty, as he said it would be. You steel yourself, don't look at the men on the plane. You don't want to seem eager or desperate or stupid. Maybe he's up front in first class, or maybe he's watching you right now. Maybe he's changing his mind. It's 3:00 A.M. Eastern Time, and scattered passengers are asleep or reading. Most of them were here when you boarded. You didn't think to check where the plane was coming from. Maybe from where he lives. Florida? Alabama?

You wait for the captain to turn the seat belt light off, and a piece of you hopes for turbulence, hopes the light will stay on and on and on until you disembark in Portland. You'll promise to reschedule but of course you won't, and—the seat belt light clicks off. He's free to move about the plane.

You do what he told you to do.

You unbuckle your seat belt and drape the flimsy airline blanket over your lap. There's no one in 34A, and you wonder if he bought that ticket, too. You push your armrests up. There are only the three seats on this side of the aisle: across the aisle an old man has fallen asleep reading the in-flight magazine. The flight attendant turns his light off as she passes.

You sit and wait.

You're wearing what he asked you to wear: the red blouse you'd told him you liked, the one that's comfortable and sexy at the same time; an underwire bra with no shoulder straps; a black skirt, short (but not too short), cut wide and loose. No stockings. No panties.

What should you be doing? Looking casual? Reading your book? Looking around? Ten minutes pass...fifteen...thirty. You wonder if you should give up, and what exactly "giving up" would entail. You wonder what you'll do when he—Someone is sitting down next to you.

You look at him, doing your best not to look nervous. He's tall, but not impressively tall, just taller than you, tall enough for that moment of awkwardness when he maneuvers his head beneath the luggage compartment to sit. Nice hands (no ring, but you don't know if it would matter). Dark blue eyes, and black wire-rimmed glasses. Light brown hair rumpled in a professorial way. Tasteful suit. No tie.

You smile, and he nods to you with an expression you can't read. You start to say something but he holds a finger to his lips and nods behind him: a businessman is sleeping in 35B. Maybe that's for the best: you have no idea what to say.

Nothing happens, for the longest time. You keep looking at him even though you don't know if you should. You don't want to seem impatient or...or you don't know what. Stupid. You don't want to seem stupid. You don't want to seem like a girl—but you want to be treated like one. Maybe.

His fingers brush your leg through the blanket. It would seem innocent if you didn't know it wasn't, like he'd just forgotten what close quarters airplanes have. You move your leg a little closer and his hand slides over it, under the blanket. He has a warm hand, with long fingers that squeeze your leg firmly, which you know is the signal.

Under the blanket you pull your skirt up, eyes studiously down; no one glancing this way could tell what you were doing.

You pull his hand between your thighs. You want him to feel that you're not wearing panties. That you shaved for him. That you did what he said.

He leans toward you, as if just getting comfortable. He pushes your thighs farther apart, and his middle fingers stroke you open, stroke you wet. You push forward, feeling the rough upholstered seat through your thin skirt. Your hand beneath the blanket caresses his for a moment.

But you pull your hand away because you don't think a caress is what he wants. You push against his hand until his finger slips into you, and when you hear the whimper in your throat as your head presses back against the seat you can't believe the sound came from you. You're not the kind of woman who makes such a noise.

Straight ahead you can see the flight attendant in that space just behind first class. You can't believe you're thousands of feet in the air with a stranger's fingers inside you and a flight attendant a few away. You could talk to her, she's that close. You could remark what an unusual thing it is for you to be sitting here with this man's fingers deep in your cunt while his palm rocks against your clit; you could explain that this really isn't an everyday thing for you, and ask, does she see it often? Is there a whole subculture of anonymous airplane sex, or is the Mile High Club couples only?

You realize suddenly that he's going to make you come, and you're struck by how ridiculous it is. And then you stop thinking at all; you focus on not groaning, closing your eyes and imagining him fucking you, imagining taking him to a hotel room in Portland and letting him fuck you—even though you promised yourself you wouldn't. You're imagining it all the same, imagining the hotel sheets against your knees, imagining raising yourself for him with your head in the pillows, so muffled you almost can't breathe. You imagine him pounding away at you with one hand on your breast and one in your hair. You imagine his hands on your ass, too, pulling you into his thrusts and grinding his hips in just the perfect way, right there, right there, right there...

His thumb is working circles against your clit. He has three fingers in you—there have never been three fingers in there before except your own—but he has three fingers in you, or maybe four, you can't tell anymore, you only know you're going to leave a wet spot on the seat.

You open your eyes and see the flight attendant again, talking to another attendant—and you make eye contact with her. She smiles, you smile back and do your best to make it innocuous. You're managing to be friendly while 34C fucks you with his hand, fills you, does your clit just right and *Oh!*—there it is, and you close your eyes again, trying not to squinch them, gulping down groans, shuddering. God, he knows you're coming! His thumb leaves your blood-engorged clit but his fingers spread you against the tightening of your muscles. Jesus god...

Everything's fuzzy for a while, and then, as you come back to yourself, you remember his rules.

You don't know how you're going to manage this. You don't look at him—you just reach over, spreading a blanket over his lap. As he pulls his hand away from you, leaving a wet trail along your thigh, you unzip his pants. He's hard and hot to the touch.

You stroke him awkwardly because you're using your wrong hand—until you twist, hoping the flight attendant will assume this is a man you're with, a man you know and love, and that you're just leaning against him affectionately. You slide your good hand under the blanket and grasp him, pulling him upward from the base, watching his lap, not his face, feeling the vein throb against your palm and listening to his breath deepen and hitch.

You grind your thighs together as you jack him off. When he's close, you dart your eyes around. No one's looking.

You pull the blanket away and drop your head. No one can see you as you take him in your mouth.

You keep your lips tightly together, forcing yourself down his shaft and up again. You keep your fingers tight around him. You stroke again, tasting the salt of him, feeling his hand twist into your hair. You rub his cockhead against the inside of your cheek and caress it with the underside of your tongue. You suck harder, panicking at the occasional wet sound your mouth makes...and then he comes. You push your face down, letting him coat the roof of your mouth and your lapping tongue.

You swallow every drop of him.

You zip him up, replace the blanket and right yourself, unable to keep from looking at him this time. He actually licks his lips.

Now you remember all the other things the two of you talked

about—what you could do in the bathroom, the reason you wore the underwire bra, and that if you lean toward 34A he can play with your ass—and the seat belt light comes on. You're on approach to Portland. It's over.

Neither of you says anything.

In the airport he squeezes your hand and walks away.

You wonder if his next flight includes another woman, if he does this all the time, if he flies around the country, fucking women in 34B.

You arrive back home at midday. His email is waiting for you.

> *Nancy—I'm so very sorry we didn't connect! My flight to Baltimore was delayed. Your plane left an hour before I arrived. Email me soon—let's make new arrangements. I'll reimburse you for the ticket if you like.*

INSTRUMENT FLIGHT RULES

Zach Lindley

I should have spent my vacation yodeling across the Alps. I had ten glorious days to take in the clean mountain air, removed from everything that lay in ruin back in the States.

Instead, I went to the little *Gasthaus* in Zweibrücken where we met when I was stationed in Germany. I listened to the native banter that I couldn't understand back then, but could now after years of marriage to a German woman. I looked deep into the room at the table where she had sat when I first saw her: long bright blonde hair framing her triangular face, vibrant blue eyes penetrating the curling billows of smoke.

The table was empty now.

I came to the *Gasthaus* from the Zweibrücken Air Force Base, which was now closed, having been decommissioned just a few years before, in 1991.

Another cold reality.

I ordered another Park Bier and listened to the beautiful song of guttural German speech before I settled in for the night at the

Erika Hotel. The room transported me back to the night we first made love; how I peeled away her clothes to reveal her voluptuous body and released the scent of expensive floral French perfume.

I drew a nice warm bath and coiled my hand tight to my cock, closed my eyes and saw Friederike's clear peaches-and-cream skin and vibrant *V* of gold pubic hair. I lingered in the tub, stroking to the edge of orgasm, then pulling back until my tortured cock burned red. I thought how I should be someplace I'd never been, clearing my head instead of stuffing it with memories. Of course, I returned to the thoughts of Friederike. A stubborn hot torrent exploded over my stomach, defying the water that had long since gone cold.

"Max Travis is on this flight?" The senior flight attendant's smile curled softly, dreamily. I'd worked with Jason before and had thought he was straight, not that it really mattered.

"Guess so." It was a last-minute change, a copilot I'd never flown with. Max was late was all I knew.

Jason swiveled on his tiptoes and peered into the boarding bridge hopefully.

I took my seat and absorbed myself in preparations. I anticipated the familiar sensation, the mild rush of takeoff. Regardless of any problems in my life, the love of flying transported me. Despite my ten days off, or perhaps in spite of them, I needed that passion now.

I'd be back in the States soon, where I could execute my elaborate plan to win Friederike back. Deep down I was realistic, but that didn't stop my formulating my plot with the same precision as that with which I'd charted the flight plan.

"Sorry I'm late." The voice was smoky, feminine, with a hint of a soft English accent.

Max Travis was a tall, athletic woman. Her skin was a warm, deep tan color, and her cheeks were dotted with large freckles. Her chestnut hair was gathered into a short ponytail. Her nose hooked downward to slender nostrils which she flared as I studied her. Full pink lips curled into a friendly smile. "I had to break every bloody speed limit."

"No problem."

Max peered over my shoulder, then circled around to the copilot's seat. "I'm Max." She reached across the pedestal and I gripped her hand. Heat emanated like a steam radiator in January.

"Dane Leonard."

"Dane? Lovely name." She joined in the preparations with a sense of authority—rapid economical movements to catch up with me. She nodded. "Sorry about the divorce."

"Pardon?"

"Sorry about the divorce."

"What makes you think—"

"Tan line on your wedding finger. That was one thick band!"

Her corneas were vibrant brown with sparkles like mica in a riverbed. There was not a trace of makeup on her face. "What makes you so sure I didn't just recently lose weight and need it resized?"

She lifted her brow.

I turned back to the instrument panel and tapped one of the displays. "Or that I lost it yodeling through the Alps?"

She smiled to reveal slightly uneven front teeth. She laughed softly.

"Or that my wife passed away?"

Her face fell serious. She angled her torso so her face was in my line of sight. "Are you telling me you didn't recently divorce?"

"Well, no."

She sat back in her seat. "It seems it was difficult for you."

"Mmm." I continued preparations.

After we lifted off from Munich, the sun lay low in the sky. We'd be chasing sunset all night.

"I love flying east to west in the evening." Max stared out over the nose of the jet.

"Me, too." I recalled how Friederike and I used to sit together to watch the sunset, and how I'd tell her that the sunset could open out below while I lingered at its edge, its descent suspended when I was traveling to the west. I recalled further how Friederike's interest in my stories of flying faded as the years wore on.

"So, how did you know I was divorced?"

"I know that look." Max tilted her head.

The lazy sun glowed a gentle orange, casting needle strips on organized waves that prepared their assault on the continent as we penetrated the coastline.

"She split with you." Not a question: a declaration.

"No."

Max leaned forward and forced her face into my line of sight. My jaw tightened. I couldn't restrain a nervous smile.

"You split with her?"

I paused then shook my head softly. "Well, no. She split with me."

"As you were 'never home?'"

"What, are you a head shrink?"

"Hardly." Max scanned the instruments.

I looked at her left hand. "Well, I don't see a tan line on *your* finger."

Max turned her head just enough that her left eye could catch me in its periphery. "The wounds will heal nicely if you'll let them. They don't all turn to scar."

* * *

Max tried to engage me in conversation from time to time. I feigned interest and gave noncommittal grunts. I got some of what she was saying. She'd lived all over, but considered Manchester, England, to be the home of her youth. She was the daughter of a distinguished pilot in the RAF and had been flying since she was a teenager. She'd fallen for and married an American soldier—ironically, an Air Traffic Controller. She did not say how it ended, just that it had and she remained in the States, a naturalized citizen. Just like Friederike, whose face I now conjured on the windshield, leading me to a hard sigh.

"So, you're formulating the plan to win her back." Max looked out over the nose of the 767. Again, not a question, but a statement. It was getting irritating.

"Of course not. We signed the final papers."

She turned her body into my line of sight the way she had each time I fed her a line. "I hope you don't fancy yourself a poker player."

I blurted a laugh and looked over my left shoulder, south over the Atlantic. She remained in position until I looked back in her eyes.

"No, I know better." My right hand was resting on the yoke, though we were on autopilot. It eased toward her. I tried to stop it, really I did, but the backs of my fingers brushed down her cheek. She was soft and smooth, and warm like a fever. My cock got heavy. I pulled my hand sharply away as if she were Sister Mary Margaret about to rap my offending knuckles.

She tilted her head curiously, then leaned back in her seat. "You have nice hands."

Sunsets vary from place to place, time to time. They are a by-product of humidity, altitude and—well, to get clinical might take the mystery and magic out of sunsets. But there are those who say that man's flying has taken the magic out of watching birds. Not true. It is the magic of flying that yields some of the most stunning sunsets. Through the malleable terrain seven miles above sea level, strips of clouds carpeted and danced with the pulsing glow of this lingering sunset.

There wasn't a trace of turbulence; it was as calm a flight as I'd ever taken—physically.

After the long, pensive silence, she rested her hand on the pedestal between us, first pretending that there was a purpose to where she had placed it. We both knew there wasn't. Still I hesitated, until she rolled her palm upward.

I laced my fingers in hers.

I hadn't gotten turned on from holding hands since Leann Dormand in eighth grade. And as powerful as that was, it didn't compare to what I felt with Max now. I had a hard-on that reverberated deep into my body. I'd never felt a need quite like it, even after long separations from Friederike in our best days when I was in the Air Force.

Max gripped tight and swallowed hard as she took me in from her peripheral vision. She held her breath when I squeezed. Her breathing became audible over the din. She turned her torso quickly over the pedestal as if it were an ambush.

It worked.

I propelled toward her despite my better judgment, like reverse thrust, hard brakes on a short runway and our teeth clicked. Her breath, tinted with ginger and orange pekoe tea, breezed into my mouth and spiced my coffee. My tongue entered her, and hers retreated coyly. The sharp points dodged and parried like fencers' foils. I grasped her strong neck with my left hand and pulled her tighter. Her clean soapy scent released with hints of her sweat. Our heads rotated in perfect time, side to side, as if we could somehow deepen the kiss like driving a screw into wood. We popped softly as my mouth left shiny prints around her lips.

"I—uh—sorry." I turned toward the instruments as if something needed attention. Something did need attention: if we were to continue and get caught, it would be an immediate dismissal.

She wiped the beads of sweat from her brow with the back of her thumb and looked away.

The autopilot controls seemed to wink at me. "Um—I was a good pilot in the Air Force."

"I believe that." Again her eye turned just enough that her dark pupil formed a tight ellipse. I realized how exceptional her peripheral vision was. The way she looked at me was extraordinarily powerful. It felt like an eye-to-eye stare from a foot away.

My hard-on had started to soften, but now it came back with a vengeance. I fumbled for words to explain. "I mean—not a great pilot. But the great ones sometimes said they'd want me on their wing in a pinch, because I was smart and reliable. They'd trust me to remain cool and make the right moves."

"Maybe you were great, and you underestimate yourself." Max smiled softly.

"No, I'm a realist. I know what I am. It's what makes me a good airline pilot."

"I bet you're a great airline pilot."

I wasn't feeling like one. I understood risks and knew how to minimize them. I calculated approaches with geometric precision. Max turned her face toward me again. Again I rubbed my fingers along her cheek. I allowed my thumb to trace her lower lip. She closed her eyes. The quiver in her breath pulsed the tip of my thumb.

I had decided long before what appealed to me in a woman:

soft, feminine curves, blonde hair, blue eyes, perfume, impeccable makeup. To get that perfect woman I'd gone to the ends of the earth in a clichéd but literal sense. To keep that perfection, I'd suffered infidelity, and forced Friederike to divorce me. My German love's passion was restrained, soft, ladylike, rationed. It was what I wanted.

It was!

The burrowing depth of Max's eyes insisted. I tried to resist, but just as my hand had explored her face on its own, my body seemed to switch to autopilot. I rose urgently and stood behind my seat. Max nodded, then followed suit. We collided, and her hand went straight down the front of my pants and gripped my rod.

I slid into her pants and split the front of her blouse, then descended into her soaked cotton panties. Our free arms, my left and her right, encircled each other like mating snakes and we shoved into each other like sumo wrestlers jockeying for control, neither yielding. We were both as silent as the reverent in an Orthodox church, the wet sound of our kisses lost in the din of the aircraft.

"We shouldn't do this, should we?" she whispered between kisses.

"I can't stop," I whispered back and kissed her ear.

"Thank god." She opened her pants and shoved them down, releasing the delicious scent of her pussy. Immediately, my pants and boxers were on the floor and we both stepped free. She turned toward the pilot's seat.

I told myself over and over that I could control this, that I could back away from her spreading thighs as she hugged the back of the seat to brace herself. The Atlantic Ocean glimmered and danced, peeking through strips of clouds below the steady nose of the 767 as my hips eased in behind her. I bent my knees to perfect my entry like the eastern approach into Lindbergh Field, just atop the rooftops in San Diego. I pushed under the tail of her shirt, Instrument Flight Rules, without the aid of guiding hands or visual confirmation. I dipped inside her perfectly. She choked on a gasp, and we moved with the rhythm of a seasoned flight team.

I gripped her shoulders like a harness. We kissed over her shoulder. Her tongue split my teeth and timed with my thrusts in her.

Ice-cold water, threat or act of dismissal, Friederike begging me to stop with the words "*Ich liebe dich*" spoken tenderly could not have parted Max and me. Desperate though I was, both in need and in fear of discovery, I lingered and fought back my swelling orgasm, knowing I might never see Max again once we had touched down and gone our separate ways.

The sun kissed the sea before us. Time seemed suspended as I released with powerful final thrusts into Max, and our silence was broken with orgasmic shouts that were both nasal and guttural.

I wondered, if the 767 had suddenly gone down, and they fished out the black box, how they would have interpreted what they heard.

I held tight to Max's back as we draped over the back of the seat and gasped for breath, but only for a moment. We recovered quickly, dressed and got back into our seats. Max produced a handkerchief and wiped her glossy brow. Our only conversations after that were in familiar flight terms.

We concluded our journey, she taking me in her peripheral vision, me fighting against fresh erections.

The approach was perfect, the landing butter smooth.

* * *

You can't get much farther from the big, wet Atlantic Ocean than the contrastingly named Sky Harbor Airport in Phoenix. I listened to the fading echoes of forward thrust to lift off. The muffled screech of tires—first contact and then second—then reverse thrust of landing. The sun descended all too fast over the desert sky; it turned the turquoise of a tropical lagoon into a sharpening strip of orange, then was gone.

The singular credentials, my enrollment in the Mile High Club, was something I'd never experience again. It was a wild ride, and an even wilder risk. But through it, I'd learned that there were risks worth taking in this life.

I had let go of Friederike some time before; in this moment, I released myself. I stirred the ice in my glass. It rang like wind chimes.

I took the last sip and let Max's tilted-head smile fill my mind. Max and I flew together twice after that sunset lingered in suspended animation. Both flights were over dry land, in the middle of the day. Both west to east, compressing the day instead of elongating it. We talked, listened and laughed, but never said a word about what had happened between us. Shortly after that, she made captain; we'd never fly together again.

The waitress looked at the scant strip of brown liquid at the bottom of my glass. "Ready for another, Cap'n?"

I was going to be in Phoenix for two days. I was in no rush to seek out the courtesy van to the hotel. I wouldn't be able to sleep anyway. "What the hell. Why not?"

"Make it two." The voice was soft and smoky, with a hint of a soft English accent. I took in deeply tanned skin and big freckles, her hair released from its usual ponytail. She looked out at an Airbus A300 taxiing out to the runway, the strip of passenger windows glistening like a zipper by candlelight. Max's wide pupils formed an ellipse. I could tell she was locked on me in her periphery. She turned her head and looked deep into my eyes. "Mind a little company? I'll be in town for a few days, and I don't fancy drinking alone."

I waved toward an open seat. "Only if we can make it more than a couple of days."

She sat down.

A BRIEF RESPITE

Desiree

I really didn't want to go but I didn't have the heart to tell him.

He looked so excited, his greenish eyes sparkling.

Our relationship wasn't working. I'd known it for some time and I believe way deep down he knew it, too, even though he seemed content in his state of denial. I guess I was mildly in denial, too. It's never easy to hurt someone.

I was nervous about spending a week at his parents' house. I was excited to see Chicago. I just hoped that I wouldn't want to throw myself out of a window before it was all over.

We were boarding the plane. I'd been very quiet and, surprisingly, he was letting me be. We'd always had trouble in this area and I was glad for the respite from his whining, no matter how brief it would be. Part of me hoped Drew would decide to stay in Chicago and not come back to New York, but I knew that wouldn't happen. The plane was tiny and that made me nervous. It kind of reminded me of that episode of "The Twilight Zone" where that ape-like gremlin was on the wing of the plane.

Before I knew it, we were seated and I felt like a death row inmate on his last walk.

I pulled my sleep mask over my eyes not because I was sleepy but to avoid any conversation with my boyfriend. I had closed my eyes for all of thirty seconds when I felt a brush against my arm. I was instantly annoyed, thinking it was Drew trying to get my attention.

"Excuse me," said a deep voice. "Are you okay?"

I started to nod, but I wanted to see who the voice belonged to so I pulled the mask off of my eyes. I almost gasped as I stared up into a pair of piercing blue eyes accompanied by a warm smile.

He was dressed head to toe in various shades of blue—a flight attendant. I was getting ready to write him off as gay but something in the way his hand lingered on my shoulder told me not to be so hasty to generalize.

"I'm fine."

The smooth caramel of his cheeks folded into two dimples as he smiled warmly and went back down the aisle. Dimples were a weakness of mine. And a brown man with blue eyes was indeed a beautiful rarity.

At least it would make for something nice to think about during the flight, I told myself. I sure as hell wouldn't be thinking of Drew unless it involved ways to break free of him.

Henry: that was the flight attendant's name. I paid extra-close attention when he demonstrated the safety procedures. I imagined that if I was drowning, his strong arms would save me. I watched him demonstrate the proper use of the seat belt and I imagined him securing my wrists with the belt as he had his way with me. When he placed the oxygen mask over his lips, I imagined that he had covered my lips with his. And when he used his fingers to motion to the emergency exits, I almost shuddered in my seat thinking of how those fingers might feel pressing into me.

I was getting wet thinking of Henry the flight attendant. So much so that I forgot I was sitting next to Drew. As Henry walked up and down the cabin, his thigh lightly grazed my arm.

We were taking off soon and Drew, in his usual gregarious manner, started to make conversation with Henry. I was annoyed. This was my piece. Drew asked him if the color of his eyes was real. I rolled mine.

"It's real," he replied, showing no sign that he'd taken offense at Drew's tacky question. I could tell the color of his eyes was genuine because I had been staring, and colored contact lenses have a decidedly fake look to them, especially in person. Henry the flight attendant looked back and forth between me and Drew. "So you're headed to Chicago," he said. "You live there?"

"My parents live there," Drew answered. "We live in New York. We're just visiting."

Henry looked amused. "So you two are a couple?"

Drew smiled widely and I almost felt bad. "Yes."

"Aww," answered Henry, looking straight at me.

It wasn't an "Oh, how cute, you two are adorable together" kind of aww. It was an "I feel badly for you. Come, let me show you what a real man is like" kind of aww.

I frowned. He didn't need to rub it in. I pulled the mask over my eyes and tried to get some sleep for real. But I wasn't sleepy. You know how you can't sleep when you're incredibly horny? My thoughts kept drifting to Henry the flight attendant: his smooth caramel skin, his deep silky voice; his wonderfully strong-looking hands. And his ass because yes, I looked. The blue uniform pants complemented his behind in a lovely way.

I looked over at Drew. I would have sucked my teeth out loud if I hadn't caught myself. Later, Henry came walking down the cabin with his beverage cart. "And what can I get for you, miss?" he cooed.

"I'll have a ginger ale."

When he handed me the cup, his fingers accidentally brushed mine. Now he was certainly flirting with me. This had to stop because it was only aggravating my condition. I gulped down my soda, hoping that the cool rush would help to curb the tingling between my legs. It didn't. We were in the first row so I could see Henry in his quarters. He was eating. He must have felt me staring at him because he looked up from his plate, put down his utensils and leaned back in his chair, eyes on me the entire time. He smiled a disarming smile and held my gaze until my eyes traveled lower and stopped on his lips just as he was bringing the lower one between his teeth. The smile widened. It was a look that said plainly, "We both know I could make you feel more pleasure than he ever could." My breath caught. I glanced over at Drew, who was in his own world, happily listening to his iPod.

I decided I needed to go to the bathroom, with the intention of getting myself off. Maybe after the release I could sleep and maybe I'd stop salivating every time I looked at Henry. I hurried to the back of the plane. The bathroom was occupied. *Shit,* I thought. It was only a few minutes, however, until the passenger came out. I went in and closed the door behind me. I undid my fly and slid my jeans down around my ankles. I dipped a finger into my pussy. I was soaking wet. I brought my finger to my nose and inhaled. I was intoxicated by the scent. I licked my finger and then circled it around my clit, letting out what I hoped was a barely audible moan. My hand was Henry's hand and he stroked my clit up and down, back and forth and in tiny circles, making my breath quicken and my nipples stand erect. I reached into my shirt and pulled out one breast, bringing the darkened bud of the nipple to my lips. I stuck my tongue out and flicked at it. My tongue was Henry's tongue, warm, hungry. I kept working at my clit with my other hand and I was shuddering, seconds away from orgasm, when there came a knock on the door.

"Are you okay?"

It was Henry's voice.

"I'm fine," I said and straightened up quickly." I'll be out in a few."

I was excited to hear his voice and at the same time annoyed at my thwarted orgasm. I felt myself blush and wondered if he knew what I was doing. The thought excited me and I quickly went back to work. I imagined opening the door and seeing him standing there. I'd make a move as if to push past him and then he'd catch my wrist in his hand and bring it to his nose. I'd feel his dick move in his pants, that's how closely to me he'd be standing and then before I knew it he'd push me back inside the bathroom.

He'd lock the door and wouldn't say a word. He'd turn me to face the wall as he reached around and unbuttoned my jeans. They'd be back around my ankles a second later. His strong hand would reach into my folds as the other cupped a breast. I'd gasp, reveling in his manly scent, his manly strength. He'd be nothing like the whiny bitch boy I was currently stuck with.

I'd reach behind me and press my hand to the front of his pants. He'd stop pawing me just long enough to undo his pants. I'd hear them drop to the floor. He'd grab my hips forcefully and push me even harder against the wall. My nipples would brush the smooth surface as they stiffened further. Cock exposed, he would press it against me and then pull my shirt up around my waist and wedge himself between my cheeks. He'd be thick. His fingers would probe me for a couple minutes and then I'd inhale a sharp breath as he plunged into me suddenly. I could practically feel the walls of my pussy stretching, struggling to accommodate his girth. My nails would dig into the bathroom wall as his dug into my hips. He'd draw all the way back and slam into me, then out and in and out and in with a force that would have me seeing stars. His fingers would sink into the flesh of my ass, holding me steady while he continued his assault.

I got so lost in my fantasy, it was like it was actually happening right then and there: His pace quickens and he's fucking me so hard and so fast, I come in record time. He places his hand over my mouth to silence me while continuing to pump forcefully inside me. I feel his legs quiver and I know he's close to the brink. I squeeze my pussy tight, clamping down on his dick, and then he bites down on my shoulder, shuddering and stifling groans as he comes inside me. He's still for a minute, waiting for our breathing to even out. He releases me from his grip, quickly does up his pants, and exits the bathroom as quietly as he'd come in.

These fantasies of Henry the flight attendant really made me take my time with myself, tease myself, make love to myself in the airplane bathroom. I pushed two fingers as far into my pussy as they would go while rubbing my clit faster with the other hand. I felt my legs quiver as I began to wonder what Henry's tongue would feel like lapping between my legs. My hand moved faster. I felt the orgasm start to rumble in my lower abdomen and I moaned. I removed my fingers from my pussy and pinched my nipple. I threw my head back and squeezed my clit between my fingers and rolled it. Then I brushed back and forth against the surface with my thumb, lightly but swiftly. My body shook as I let out a guttural sound and I had to brace my foot against the wall to steady myself. After letting my breathing return to normal, I fixed my clothes and washed my hands. Then I tried to wipe the stupid grin off my face.

I exited the bathroom, half expecting my fellow passengers to shoot scandalized looks my way and point judgmental fingers. But no one seemed to notice me as I made my way back to my seat, where Drew was happily listening to jazz on his iPod, right where I left him.

"Are you okay?" he asked as I sat down.

I grinned widely. "I'm fine," I said.

"Good." He smiled. "I'm glad you're in a better mood. We'll have fun, you'll see."

"I don't doubt it," I said. I took one last glance over at Henry, smiled, and then pulled my sleep mask back over my eyes to finally settle in for a nap.

GET ON, GET OFF

Jeremy Edwards

Get on, get off when you fly in masturbation class! Only from Zirbin Airlines.

Trendsetting tycoon Maxwell Zirbin had definitely outdone himself this time. Granted, his enormously successful business plan for the airline that bore his name had always hinged on the sorts of innovations that hip consumers would find seductive—in an industry otherwise noted for dreariness and inconvenience, served up in three shades of blah. From the retro-chic color schemes to the sensory overload of onboard entertainment to the sassy personalities of the cabin crew, the word *Zirbin* had become synonymous with airborne fun.

Even in this context, the introduction of a special, sequestered seating section (eighteen-plus) for passengers who wanted the comfort, release, or diversion of being able to masturbate en route from New York to London was considered pretty damn daring. It was one thing to be plied with Day-Glo cocktails by charming, androgynous flight attendants who danced their way down the aisle to house music; it was quite another to be informed at check-in that one could upgrade to wanking class for only a fifty dollar surcharge.

"We have plenty of seating available in Zirbin M-Class," the agent told Jared discreetly. Jared remembered reading that this latest Zirbin revolution, although it had understandably attracted plenty of publicity, was only beginning to catch on with passengers.

Jared represented the target audience well. High on libido and low on inhibitions, he found lengthy plane rides boring as hell. Long before Zirbin had unveiled M-Class, it had occurred to Jared that a nice, sensuous stroke session would be a great way to refresh and relax himself at about hour five of a transatlantic jaunt. And he could see why the possibility would appeal to others, too—to the retiree whose flame had been kindled by an ocean-side torso in her travel guide, or by a lingering look at the tight-trousered crew member who'd offered her a pillow; to the macho guy whose only phobia was flying, and who could use one more thing to take his mind off the altitude; to the overworked, overtraveled executive woman who might be so very glad to undo the knot of tension between her legs.

He handed over the fifty bucks, and the agent asked for his seating preference: "Male neighbor, female neighbor, or no preference?" The seats were two abreast in M-Class—with a retractable curtain between them—and your neighbor would, at a minimum, be the person you were most likely to sense, and whose motion might make your own seat vibrate in sympathy.

"Female," Jared responded, feeling a tingle in his groin.

"All set, sir. You understand that the curtain between seats goes up only by mutual consent?"

"Yes, of course."

* * *

The seats were certainly very comfortable. This in itself, Jared observed, might have been worth the extra fifty. Still, there was no doubt in his mind that he intended to get his money's worth out of the premium price, in every way.

M-Class was on the upper deck of the plane. The seats were all on one side of the aisle, with a row of utility cupboards lining the other side. Jared, who'd been assigned the outside seat, got himself situated and pulled the outside curtain closed. He had noted, with a bit of disappointment, that his neighbor had already taken her place and closed the interior curtain between them—meaning that he probably wouldn't get a chance to see what she looked like until such time as she got up to use the lavatory, or peeked out to accept a drink or a snack. (Surely, Jared reasoned, one got drinks and snacks in masturbation class.)

He glanced down to take in his companion's feet—the only part of her not concealed by the curtain. She wore beige stockings, and black shoes with a low heel. There was nothing very distinctive about these details, but nonetheless Jared searched his brain for recollections of women he might have noticed in the departure lounge, to see if he could put a face to these feet. But he came up blank. The plane had boarded very soon after he'd upgraded, and he hadn't had the time or the focus to make a study of his fellow passengers. The only woman he happened to remember, a redhead with a pleasant, quasi-permanent smirk, had been wearing sleek pink and white sweats with running shoes. By default, Jared's mind automatically planted that woman's face atop the mostly invisible body seated to his right, though he knew it wasn't the same person.

He was reluctant to speak to her through the curtain—unless she spoke to him first. Instead, he quietly wondered if she'd specifically requested a male neighbor, or if she'd had no preference. Would she actually have preferred to be entirely alone? Or maybe part of what had made her select M-Class had been the opportunity to do herself with a stranger just inches away—someone like him. This thought gave Jared the beginning of his official masturbation-class erection.

He tried to relax. Airline regulations clearly stated that masturbation was not to occur during takeoff or landing. For a moment, he wondered why. Then he realized that, of course, it was the seat belt issue. He visualized an urgently horny but rule-abiding passenger hiking her skirt up to access herself during takeoff, while still keeping her belt buckled. Then he imagined the woman next to him doing that.

The image made his erection burgeon further—even before he saw a pair of black silk panties float down to his neighbor's ankles, sort of like the oxygen masks that always pop down in the safety videos.

"*Mmm.*" The sound he heard from the seat beyond the curtain was soft, but unmistakable. Even amid the moderate hubbub of flight attendants clattering around, passengers settling into place, engines warming up, and air-conditioning cycling on, her purr of light pleasure came across loud and clear. Jared's neighbor, having slipped her panties down, was obviously getting into the mood. He imagined her shifting her hips and squeezing her thighs together for a second before touching the exposed flesh under her skirt.

Jared was the rule-abiding sort himself, but he figured there was no harm in unzipping his fly while they awaited takeoff. It felt good to do so. He let his hand rest firmly on the opening in his jeans, and he found his hearing tuned keenly toward the neighboring seat.

Things went smoothly for the flight crew, and it couldn't have been more than fifteen minutes before they'd taxied, soared, and leveled off. But cruising altitude came none too soon for Jared, whose cock, still enclosed by a thin layer of underwear, pulsed tentatively but unceasingly against his palm. The woman, his partner, was clearly biding her time as well; Jared heard no further sounds from her while they ascended, and the elegant feet remained still, looking like a piece of lewd sculpture with the panties seductively adorning them. It crossed his mind that this must be what one woman sees of another in neighboring bathroom stalls—shoes and panties. Almost involuntarily, he visualized the long row of stalls in an airport women's room, then visualized the row of soft, bare asses inside those stalls, each neatly seated for that satisfying postflight pee. His cock ached, and he gave it a sustaining squeeze.

At last, the pilot switched off Zirbin's trademark FASTEN SEATBELTS sign—a cartoon crocodile in sunglasses, whose 1970s-style belt and buckle appeared to be part of his body. Even as Jared registered this, he heard a deep, sensual sigh from next door, and he could only assume that his invisible companion's fingers had made welcome contact with her intimate zone.

He extricated his cock from his briefs, letting out a silent sigh of his own as his fist finally met his flesh. At least he thought it had been silent, but a peculiar discontinuity in the breathing from beyond the curtain made him feel that his partner had heard him, and had tracked his progress. It excited him to speculate that she was that aware of him, as she gently nurtured her hungry pussy lips.

He squirmed in his seat, and he accidentally brushed the curtain. For an instant, he felt the solidity of the body on the other side.

"Sorry." He whispered it.

"Okay," returned a breathy voice, raw with intensity.

The voice, that aroused *"Okay,"* echoed in his head as he

stroked himself. Its imagined repetition became a masturbation mantra, blending with the real sound of the jet—and the real sounds coming from lap and mouth level one seat over. Her wetness was now audible, and Jared could visualize the slippery activity of delicate fingers across and between pouting lips, as vividly as if it were being displayed for him on Zirbin's egg-shaped video screens. As her breathing dipped, plodded, and crested to a complex and ever-changing rhythm, he thought he could actually follow her trail along her folds, in and out of her cunt, and back and forth to her clit. His own rhythm, simple but powerful, rocked him in harmony with her.

He reached for one of the generous, Zirbin-monogrammed handkerchiefs, which were provided within a candy-striped Personal Intimacy Kit that also included plastic bags, disinfecting gel, and—just in case people wanted to join forces—a box of condoms. With a grape-colored handkerchief wrapped around him, he gave out a prehistoric grunt.

"*Hey,*" the breathy voice suddenly said, in a labored whisper rich with erotic texture.

"Yeah?" Jared was tingling right on the edge.

"*Maybe we could pull the curtain up.*"

It was technically a "maybe" statement rather than an invitation, but Jared knew what it meant. Clutching his swaddled cock in his left hand, he used his right, with passionate dexterity, to release the catch that had kept the curtain anchored. With a *shoooop* of relief, it disappeared into a slit in the ceiling—leaving only a plastic nipple visible, by means of which future passengers would, at some far-off time, pull it back down.

The face that greeted him was a tableau of melting, sensuous beauty. The woman's blonde hair was in disarray, her eyes were glazed in preorgasmic semifocus, and her mouth twitched in a way that made her lip gloss repeatedly catch, and transform, the sterile cabin light. Her white blouse was unbuttoned enough to show two cheerful breasts, each half-out of its bra cup, with nipples erect and moistened.

She was so far gone down the road to ecstasy that Jared couldn't tell what she might look like in repose, what expression her face would hold under normal circumstances. But here, now, she was stunning—possessed of that quintessential grace that comes to a woman on the verge of orgasm.

She smiled at him, then closed her eyes.

He realized that a moment of eye contact with him—enabling her to observe that his gaze was on her exuberant breasts, on her hiked black skirt, on her cunt-clutching fingers, and, most important of all, on her radiant face—had been all she needed to go over the top. Now she threw her head back as far as the seat in its fully upright position would allow, and she quivered, absolutely quivered, from panty-draped ankles to self-mussed hair. Her moan sounded all the more intense for its courteous softness.

And Jared got his money's worth out of Maxwell Zirbin's big purple handkerchief. He pumped for what seemed like forever as he inhaled her aroma, contorted his eyes shut, and visualized a night sky of milky clouds over the Atlantic.

Just when he had milked himself dry, he heard her voice again.

"Want a taste?" She sounded shy, but somehow confident. He opened his eyes. Her fingers, held aloft, were glistening, and her pupils were sparkling.

Without hesitation, he leaned forward and sucked one finger, then another, then another.

"Nice," he commented, feeling suddenly drunk with impetuousness, and completely at ease. "You taste like berries. And maybe, uh, tamari. And—mm—a hint of black pepper." He licked his lips.

She laughed. "Thanks. But I think you may have read one too many of *Zirbin Magazine*'s extreme wine columns."

He joined her laughter. "Well, yeah, it's possible."

"Just don't tell me I taste like cilantro. I hate cilantro."

"Deal."

They laughed again, and Jared noticed that she was perhaps even lovelier when she laughed than when she came. He wanted to see more of both.

Thank god it was going to be a long flight.

THE SCREAM QUEEN

Sommer Marsden

I couldn't resist. It was only ten minutes into the flight when I leaned in and said the inevitable, "Hey, aren't you...?" Then I stammered, embarrassed at my fandom.

"Jannie Blair. Yes. Guilty as charged." Her hair was close cropped and alternating shades of dark gray and silver. Her blue eyes sparkled. She smiled and incredibly white teeth shone behind full, mauve-painted lips: gorgeous. I crossed my legs and flexed my thighs, but it did no good. It didn't stifle a damn thing. My crush on her reared up, bright and shining and feeling brand new instead of twenty years old.

"God. Not to sound like a babbling idiot but I loved you in *All Saint's Eve*. Edna, your trained parrot, too. My god! You were so sexy in that movie," I gushed. I wanted to shut my damn mouth but it wouldn't stop. I could hear myself, as if from a great distance, rattling off favorite movies and characters, and dear god help me, wardrobe choices. "That blue dress was so incredible. I have tried and tried to find a dress that makes my tits look that good and I can't." Then my face was scorching red and I swallowed. I had just said the word *tits* to Jannie Blair. "Maybe I just don't have the tits."

Damn it. It was getting worse.

"Your tits are very nice. Don't be that way," she said. Her eyes were a shiny bold blue and her laugh was easy; sensual and captivating, just like in the movies. "I'd say you have a lovely pair there...um...?"

"Judith. Judith Montgomery. I work for Suncoast Studios. *Dames of the Dead*, that's one of mine. I'm sure you've never seen it. Really. I think four people saw it and you were not one of them. Of that I am almost positive." I took a huge swig of scalding hot coffee to shut myself up. I wasn't sure, but it felt as if a whole row of blisters had just blossomed on the roof of my mouth.

She laughed and then put her hand on my thigh and squeezed. I looked at her hand to make sure the sensation was genuine. Yep. There it was, on my thigh. Her hand, all long fingers and red manicure, rested on my thigh, squeezing my leg through my black pencil skirt. "Don't be so sure. My youngest son is nineteen. It just so happens that *Dames of the Dead* is one of his favorites."

"I..." I flexed my thigh under her hand and she squeezed again. Then her thin hand slid higher and she squeezed my upper thigh. I felt a warm trickle of fluid in the crotch of my sensible black cotton panties. I closed my eyes, then opened them. Her hand was still there. I was not hallucinating.

"Darla, they'll eat you...alive!" she recited.

"That's Baby Cathy's line!" I said, excited and shocked. She wasn't just bullshitting me. She had seen the movie.

Jannie nodded and leaned in closer. When she leaned in, her breasts pushed up high in her tight black dress. Her cleavage seemed a mile deep and I fought the mental image of sliding my tongue along the seam of flesh, burrowing my tongue into that cleavage and then finding a sweet blush-colored nipple to taste.

"I told you. Chuckie has watched that movie about a billion times, and I've watched it at least a dozen times. It's hard not to. The birthday cake scene is the best."

"Eew!" I laughed, though. A birthday cake adorned with flaming fingers instead of candles was a hard image to shake. Almost as hard as Jannie Blair's naked thighs in *The Sun Sets Blood Red* in 1977. Or her shower scene in *My Deadly Darling* at the end of her career. When Jenson Belmar fucked her blue in the shower as Kelly Dubois kneeled in front of her. It was not only a killer zombie movie, but that was a killer threeway scene, one of the first, and she had been in it. I had always wondered about her after that scene.

Turbulence rocked us and I thought that was bad, so soon into the flight. Not good at all. "Jesus."

"You don't like to fly?" Her breath was hot along my neck and for a moment I forgot about the turbulence and just wanted to kiss her.

"Not so much. Not a big fan, actually. But business is business and I'm flying out to scout a location in New York and..." I shrugged.

"My hometown." She said the words right against my earlobe and the vibration meandered down my belly to my pussy. I shifted in the cramped airplane seat and felt the seat belt rub my belly in a not unpleasant way.

I cleared my throat and reminded myself who this woman was. Jannie Blair was not interested in me. I was suffering from delusions of grandeur. She was one of the premier slasher sirens. She had screamed with the best of them and had made blood and terror sexy. She had thoroughly earned her name, the Scream Queen. I shifted. "Have you been to Rico's? That's what

I'm looking at. We're shooting a huge vampire smack down in Rico's. The stonework and gargoyles are amazing. At least from the photos I've seen."

"They are." The words were no sooner out of her mouth than she leaned in and nipped my ear. I gave a little cry and her hand moved just a fraction of an inch higher on my leg.

"Oh. Good. I..." I what? I had no idea. My brain had short-circuited and my body had hijacked all sensation. My heart was banging restlessly and my pulse jumped in my neck. I shook my head because I felt dizzy and the plane jumped, making it that much worse.

"I like your skirt. It's what a real woman would wear," she said. Her breath smelled like chocolate.

"I'm sorry?"

"Oh. Don't be." She laughed at her own joke and the crow's feet at the corners of her big blue eyes deepened. There was something sexy about how they made her bright blue eyes even brighter. "What I mean is, I watch all these professional women walking around dressed like teenagers. This is beyond sexy, this skirt. And it shows off your hips."

Yeah. My hips. I wasn't too crazy about my hips. But I was starting to think the whole shower scene had been fairly accurate. She was flirting with me. "Thanks. Thank you." Then before I could still my tongue, I blurted, "I have to pee."

And I did. Nerves had gotten the better of me. The flirting wasn't helping. Years of fantasizing about this particular woman had set me on edge. Here we sat, side by side, and she had just bitten my earlobe. Her hand was on my thigh. I was thousands of miles in the air and the flight was a bit turbulent. And I had to pee.

"This is a nice plane," she said. "They have big bathrooms. Big enough for two."

I had finally caught on. I had no doubt that Jannie Blair had just offered to join me in the restroom. I stood and she steadied me when the plane rocked and tilted. Normally, terror would have ripped through me but excitement served as a distraction. I took my time moving down the aisle, working my way from seat to seat.

"Miss, you'll have to take your seat," the flight attendant said.

"I'm really not well." I was only half lying. My stomach had just done a nice loopdy loop and I wondered which emotion would win, fear or arousal.

"Miss, please." I could hear the frustration in his voice. He frowned at me and bit his bottom lip. His bright red hair stood up in tufts from his having run his hands through it in frustration. I didn't budge, but stood my ground in the narrow aisle. "Look, if I let you go, will you promise to come right back? Quickly. People are freaking out left and right and truth be told, if you are careful and hold on in the bathroom, you should be fine. Just keep your hand on something. Stay steady."

I nodded slowly and the plane did an unexpected dip. My stomach bottomed out and I swallowed a whoop of surprise.

"They're afraid people will lose their balance and fall or hit their heads or..." Someone in the front of the plane started to cry and he sighed. "Just hurry, okay?"

I nodded again and walked the remaining distance to the restroom on numb legs. I heard him speak again and then heard Jannie's calm smoky voice say, "I'm with her. I have her medicine." I knew exactly what I would have my hands on to keep me steady.

I smiled when he chirped, "Yes, Ms. Blair!" There was something to be said for slasher stardom.

I had time to register that she was right about the bathroom size. That was all. My eyes took in the chrome room and the extrawide shelf area for your bag or purse. I got all that at a glance and then I heard the door and Jannie was on me, aggressive and quick. I laughed a little even as my heart seized up in my chest. She pinned me face-first to the pebbled silver wall and shoved her slim, cool hands down the front of my skirt. "You are wondering about the shower scene. Or you have," she said in my ear.

I nodded. "Yes. I have. But I bet everyone, boy or girl, who's ever crushed on you has wondered."

"It is the number one question." Her fingers slid under the waistband of my panties and I closed my eyes and tried to breathe. She was so close and I still couldn't quite believe it was real. That she was about to touch me there.

"I'm sure," I gasped. Her fingertip parted my outer lips and I watched my unsteady breath fog up the chrome in front of my lips. Jannie rolled a tight circle over my clit and my knees went a little loose.

"It was real. Don't tell. It's a secret. To this day, most people in the industry believe it was staged," she said coolly, working harder and harder circles as I chugged closer and closer to orgasm. I splayed my fingers on the cool wall and rested my cheek there, too. I couldn't seem to get enough air but I listened. "Only a select few of us knew. He was really fucking me, she was really sucking me, and the unsteady shot toward the end was because Buzzy the camera guy got off at the same time I did."

"Oh." My voice was a few octaves higher than normal as I clawed at the wall. Jesus. But Jesus couldn't help me now. I was in the hands of Jannie Blair and I was about a gnat's ass away from coming like a freight train.

"So basically it was porn but it made it to the big screen. Or as big as B movies get." I felt the button at the back of my skirt give and she tugged the zipper. Her other hand joined the first and she slid two perfectly manicured fingers into my wet pussy. I sagged back against her and she nibbled the back of my neck. My nipples pebbled and my skin followed suit.

"They always blurred it out, sadly," I said, laughing, and felt my pussy clench around her fingers. I was pretty much done for. I put my lips to my forearms to stifle myself.

The plane bobbed and weaved and I wondered what would happen if we fell in a tangled injured heap on the floor. What a mess that would be. What a scandal.

Her laugh was throaty. "I know. But I have an unedited copy at home. If you'd like to see it when we land. My sons are with their father and I could use the company."

Her fingers slipped in and out of me effortlessly. I was beyond wet. I could hear the slick sounds of her fingers fucking me and the rustle of my skirt seemed louder than the plane. "I'd like that!" I bit my forearm as my cunt spasmed around her fingers. She fucked me harder and juices seeped down my inner thighs, warm and wet. Another warm wave rolled through me and I bucked in her arms. The plane wobbled.

"Good girl. Even through your fear you gave me such a nice one," she whispered against my throat.

"You. I want you," I said, turning. "Before that redheaded flight attendant shows up and starts banging on the door. He'll notice we're not back. He will." I moved her back as I chattered anxiously, my skirt hanging loosely around my hips.

I pushed her until her hips connected with the chrome counter. Her dress was long and black, tucked and tailored at her waist but with a voluminous skirt. I burrowed under it desperately until she helped me out by bunching it at her waist. I didn't think about the fact that I was kneeling in an airplane bathroom. I could Handi-Wipe my knees later. She made a small noise and I pushed her black lace panties down: tango pants. No thong for her; classy grown-up panties instead.

Her thighs were softer than once upon a time and pale white. She smelled like spices and arousal and lavender. I touched my tongue to her clit and she hissed. I licked harder, sucking the essence of her into my mouth. She tasted like flowers. The plane tilted to the left and we both slid just a bit. I knew he'd come looking: that attendant. I could feel the excitement of limited time run up my spine. I shivered. Jannie plunged her hands into my hair as I shoved my rigid tongue into her wet pussy.

Her short pubic hair tickled my nose and I nudged her harder, suckling until I thought I might suffocate. Her fingers found my nipples and she pinched me. I bit her clit gently and she let out a high cry that made me think of her movies.

I worked my fingers inside of her and stroked her swollen G-spot. She was so ready, my fingertips went right to it and I teased it with my fingertips. Another tilt and we slid to the right. "You have to hurry, Jannie," I said. "He's coming. I'm sure of it."

I clamped my lips back over her hot little clit and sucked. I finger-fucked her furiously as she pulled my hair in short yanks. I felt her cunt seize up around my fingers and I laughed for just a moment. "Oh, god...god, god!" Jannie yelled. But true to movie form, she kept gathering steam as she came, letting loose with a high earsplitting shriek as the orgasm ripped through her.

Sharp knuckles rapped the door and a muffled voice yelled, "Is everything okay in there? Do you need help?"

It was my redheaded friend. "No," I called, stifling a laugh, "Just scared by the turbulence. It's fine!" Then I stood unsteadily and kissed Jannie's full lips. "Lady, you really are the Scream Queen."

"Sweetie, you ain't heard nothing yet," she said and kissed the tip of my nose.

WILD CHILD

Matt Conklin

Sex on planes is stupid. These people think they're so cool for joining the "Mile High Club." They probably think that sneaking a joint makes them oh so rebellious too. Whatever. Fucking on airplanes is overrated. They're just dumb conformists who want to do it because they read about it in a magazine. I just want to get to L.A. already. This whole thing is stupid....

I couldn't help looking over her shoulder. She was sitting right next to me, after all, and I've never been one not to notice a woman, even if she is fifteen years my junior. But even if I weren't the type to try to see what my seatmate was reading or check her out, the furious way this girl was scribbling in her notebook, a loud, angry kind of scrawl, was the equivalent of pounding a piano keyboard, hard, and it was difficult to ignore.

Her entire aura was angry, and she was dressed in typical

post-teen fashion—black tank top over jeans, with a black hoodie, plenty of black eyeliner, an eyebrow ring, and a scowl. Oh, and dark green Converse sneakers. As I took in her words, I knew immediately that she was all but a virgin. She was too fired up, too cocky to have ever fully surrendered to a boy—or a girl. She had all the charm of a young woman whose sensuality is hidden not so deeply beneath the surface, but who just hasn't figured it out yet.

She made me want to smack some sense into her, or fuck her. I could've told her to grow up, but what would be the point? So she could become jaded, I mean, "mature," like me? No, I figured I could have some fun with her, though, and maybe let Miss Attitude know that there's more than one way to get screwed on an airplane.

Her eyes, once you got past the shaggy bangs and overdone makeup, were almost sexy. And yes, I was now officially a dirty old man, likely twice her age or damn close, for even considering what she had going on under that hoodie. But she started it, and I felt like it was in both our best interests to pursue it.

"You're wrong, you know," I said in as snotty a voice as I could muster. Like meets like and all that. "It's not just about yuppies sneaking off for a quickie and calling it the best sex of the year. There are all kinds of ways to fuck on a plane. You're just too young to know about them."

She glared up at me, and let me tell you, it was the sexiest glare I'd ever seen, the kind of sneer that says "Leave me alone" and "I want to suck your cock" at the very same time, the kind of stare that made my dick even harder. "Like you'd know," she muttered, then cut me with her eyes before turning to face the window, deliberately closing her journal and curling up into a ball as best she could within the confines of the seat. Normally, I don't care what my neighbors are reading or eating or doing on a plane; I'm intent on getting where I'm going as quickly as possible. I've had my share of fun on planes, but for the most part I think they're utilitarian vehicles, the fastest way to get from point *A* to point *B*, nothing to get too excited about.

But I was excited about this girl, because she was definitely a girl, not a woman—not even close. I'd been spending my time with women who'd been around the block, who knew exactly how to give a blow job designed to make me melt, who approached sex like a sport they'd already won several medals in. Maybe that's not totally fair, but I was bored. I was on the plane because I wanted to shake things up, not necessarily with a wild fling, but with something different. I'd been certain a quick trip to Miami would snap me out of my rut. I'd fantasized about somewhere more exotic, but time was even tighter than money and I just wanted to be in the sun, soak up a few rays, ogle some chicks in bikinis and flirt and drink and not think about my latest breakup or my job performance. Things were salvageable at work, but I wasn't exactly going to be made employee of the year. I'd been drinking too much and had taken some of my frustration out on Heather, who'd finally had enough. But looking at this girl full of smoldering sex appeal buried beneath layers of goth indifference, I wondered if maybe I didn't even need to get to the land of beaches, sunshine, and Cuban flair for that to happen. This wild child seemed tailor-made for that, and looked like she could use someone to talk some sense into her before she became jaded like all the others.

Just then the stewardess came by and asked about drinks. My companion surprised me by ordering a club soda. I opted for water—with extra ice, and a whiskey. I smiled politely even as my mind formed deviant plans. My seatmate continued to pretend to ignore me, but I sensed her eyes peering at me over her shoulder. I pulled out a book, some thick thriller on the bestseller list I'd grabbed off the shelves. I used to have a stack of books just waiting to be read, and would sometimes rush home to them like they were old friends, but lately all I'd been reading were labels on jars and captions on my TV screen.

I tried to act like I was immersed in the book, playing hard to get, if you will, but when the stewardess returned with my requested cup of ice, I was grateful for the chance to pull out my tray, and grinned up at her. I think she thought I was flirting with her, from the way she leaned down, thrusting her tits in my face. That brief nearness made my seatmate a little jealous, apparently, because she scowled at the woman and demanded both a Coke and a tomato juice. "You better not spill on me," I said to her like she was eight.

"Why don't you just mind your own business?" she snapped back.

"Are you sure that's really what you want...Donna?" I asked, having copped a glance at the copy of *Bust* with its address label still attached she'd been rifling through.

"You're damn nosy, you know that?"

"You were the one writing about something that I happen to have a vested interest in."

"I was writing in my *journal,* you idiot."

"Fine. Stay young and uninformed, I don't care," I said, sipping the whisky I'd so wisely had the busty stewardess bring me. I reached for my book again and tried to imagine I was in first class. But my cock was insistent that I not let this one get away.

I ignored her for as long as I could stand it before turning toward her. She now had her headphones on full blast, her hoodie hiked up around her ears, and her body turned all the way away from me, her petite build allowing her to sit with her legs tucked against her as she faced the window, staring into the darkening sky.

"The ice is melting. Such a shame," I said quietly.

"Why?" She wasn't exactly gracious, but I was pretty sure I had piqued her interest.

"I don't know. Some people, you know, those stuffy, uptight dickwads you think so highly of, might be interested in playing with ice, like a sex toy. I'm sure that would be way beneath you, so there's no point in even going on about it."

There was silence for a few minutes as I sipped my drink and actually let myself get sucked into the mystery novel, the first clues making my brain spin with possibilities. Just when I thought I had a lead on who the killer might be, she spoke again. "Not that I actually care or anything, but what exactly would you do with the ice? And how do you do it without getting caught?"

I turned to look at her and her eyes seemed wider, the makeup seeming to fade as she stared up at me. "Well, the only real way to tell you is to show you. Otherwise it'll just sound boring. Do you think you're up for it? I'm not so sure a delicate flower like you could stand it. It's really more for the...masochistic sort of girl." Of course I already knew that she was as submissive as they come. It's the bratty ones who always need a good spanking, and the sniveling, simpering ones who are actually the biggest bitches once you scratch that outer layer. Time and time again, my theory has been proven right, as ballsy babes who've busted my nuts at work or among friends have begged to have their hair pulled, to choke on my cock, to be degraded in ways even I hadn't thought of.

Donna looked up at me and nodded. "I can take it." She said it like I was about to take her before a firing squad, rather than make her more aware of her nipples than she'd ever been.

"Try not to sound too enthusiastic," I said right into her ear. She shivered, and I made my lips brush against her lobe. "Cold?"

"No, I'm fine," she said.

"Good, because you're about to get a lot colder." And with a practiced move, I took one of the pieces of ice in my hand, put my arm around her, and quickly worked it below her T-shirt and into her bra. I made sure it was secure there, as I felt it start to melt just a little. I allowed my fingers only a brief meeting with her already-hardening flesh before removing my hand and patting her on the shoulder.

She looked at me again, her mouth open, fishlike. "Don't say anything. It's better that way. Just take deep breaths and focus on the sensation. And get used to it because I'm about to add another one," I told her. Her face could not have looked more shocked. Having ice melting against your nipples is one of those things you can't really prepare for. Even if you think you know what you're getting into, the reality is more painful, chilling, and exciting than you could have expected.

"Yes, there's going to be another one...unless you can tell me you hate it. Can't stand it. Wish I hadn't done it." The more I talked, the faster the words bubbled out, the stiffer my cock got. I'd wanted to try to play it cool, but I was just as aroused as she was. Initiation should be its own fetish, its own niche in the world of sex. Watching a woman go from barely knowing where her clit was to realizing that her nipples were way more sensitive than she'd thought, and could take all sorts of torment, was as beautiful as watching the glorious sunset going on outside our window.

"No. I mean, I can't say that. I don't know...I wouldn't say I like it, but I'd be disappointed if you didn't do it again."

"How disappointed?" I asked, stroking her cheek with one rough thumb.

"Well...I'd think you were a big, mean bully," she said. Now she was just toying with me.

"But would that really be such a bad thing?" I asked her before reaching down to pinch her icy nipple. She let out a sigh, then a hiss, as I manipulated the ice through the fabric of her T-shirt and hoodie so it was more directly in contact with her nipple.

"Oh, Donna, this is only the beginning. Because in a little while, I'm going to hand you three pieces of ice and tell you to go to the bathroom and insert them inside your pussy. And yes, you're going to do it, then walk back here, sit down, and make a big puddle in your seat. It's going to look like you've peed your pants. You're going to almost wish you *had* peed your pants, that it had all been an accident, because even though the ice is cold, your pussy's going to be on fire." I let my words sink into her stubborn little brain.

"But what about you?" she asked, clearly stalling for time.

"What about me?" I asked back, even though one look down at my crotch revealed just how hard this discussion was making me.

"I mean, why do I have to be the one to suffer? Don't you get to be iced up too?"

"Oh, little girl..." I said, then reached between her legs so she could feel my heat and I could feel hers. "There's so much you still have to learn. That is, if I'm not boring you by being a, what was it...?" I paused and shifted my fingers. "Oh yeah, a 'dumb conformist,'" I said as I pressed my palm flush with her pussy.

"No, you're not. You're not, I promise. I didn't know," she said, then clutched my arm tightly.

"What didn't you know, Donna?" I asked calmly as I plucked another piece of ice out of the rapidly melting pile and put it in my mouth. I held it between my teeth and smiled at her, waiting for her answer.

"I didn't know it would feel this good, or that I'd get so

turned on. I've only been with one guy, Rich, my ex-boyfriend. He was always all about the in-and-out—he said anything fancier was dreamed up by people with nothing better to do, who were never going to change the world."

"Ah, my dear, that's where you're wrong. If anything's going to change the world, it's going to be sex." I pried her fingers off my arm. "I think you need some more ice cubes," I told her.

She didn't object, didn't shrink away or glare. She watched, her eyes glued to my hand, as I took another cube and quickly slipped my hand down her shirt and into her bra, dropping my little gift, then extricating myself. My wet fingers dripped onto her neck as I massaged it.

"Now you," I said. "Rub it directly against your nipple. Think about what I could do if I had you alone, your breasts hanging out of your bra, your nipples straining in the air." Silently, she held one hand over her breast, using her hoodie to massage it into her. "After that melts, it'll be time for you to go to the bathroom," I whispered. She didn't say a word, but her shudder said it all. If you're tuned in to body language, a careful movie-watcher, a reader of the book of humanity, you can tell a shudder of horror from one of pleasure. They are oceans apart, gestures similar only in name. This shudder said, "I never thought it could feel this good. I don't care that we're on a plane, who knows how many feet in the air, in public, strangers. I just want more." Watching Donna was a pleasure all its own, a visual feast as my words and fingers coordinated to untangle her, unwrap her, unleash her. I, too, was changing, from dirty old man to enraptured seducer, her pleasure humming through my body as if we were attached by a wire.

"I bet you're very wet right now. I bet you're not thinking about how fast this plane is flying so it can get you to Miami and away from me."

"No...I'm not." There was a pause, while I breathed against her neck, out, then in, inhaling her scent, musky and flowery at once. "I like this," she said quietly. It was a simple statement, and from someone else might've been a small admission. But from her, it was everything. I had her. I cupped her pussy once more through her jeans, grinding my palm against it. She sunk lower in her seat, pressing back against me.

I leaned over and pressed my forehead lightly against hers, kissed her cheek softly. Kissing on planes is highly underrated. My lips met the soft skin of her cheek and I was reminded of just how young she was, her skin perfectly smooth, so tender I could practically sink right inside it, full of promise. I was too old for her in real life, whatever that was, but here, on this plane, I didn't mind making her feel hot and cold and aroused and wanted for a little while. She turned toward me and our lips met tenderly, like two teenagers making out in a movie theater, even as the ice wet her shirt and her pussy begged for more.

Her tongue insisted on entering my mouth, though her movements were small and tentative at first. I let her explore me before grabbing her hair and shoving my tongue into her mouth, as quietly as I could, the invasion swift, decisive. I knew our fellow passengers had to notice something amiss. It's hard to ignore two people in the throes of passion; even if you think you're not listening or observing, those telltale shifts, those familiar sounds rise up into your consciousness. I reminded myself that for all these people knew, she was my wife—my very young trophy wife, with me cast as the dirty old perv.

I didn't mind though, and when we broke apart, panting, I held my hand to her lips. She kissed each finger in turn, then unbuckled her seat belt and slithered over me, making sure to pause when her legs were straddling mine, a look on her face that, for a moment, made me question whether she was, indeed, as innocent as I'd painted her in my mind. She reached into the cup of ice and grabbed a handful, then winced as the shock of its cold sting greeted her. Then, still poised above me, Donna took a piece of ice and traced it over my lips, making them tremble, then part. She pressed it against my tongue and it felt heavy, solid.

She didn't want to be in charge, I could tell, but she wanted to at least let me know she could be. Then she turned and walked toward the back of the plane.

I swallowed hard. When she'd been right in front of me, I could easily let myself forget our surroundings. With her gone, I tried my best to stare straight at my hand, examining imaginary hangnails, my cuticles, my skin, memorizing the hairs on my knuckles. I was embarrassed, a new emotion for me. I didn't ask myself whether it was wrong to corrupt her, whether I should have waited for some other clueless kid her age who'd maybe banged one chick to show her what she was missing.

I was too horny for that. Her virginal yet knowing body was already haunting me. It had been, what, five years—or maybe more—since I'd been with a girl who was truly innocent, almost ignorant, about sex. Showing her not only how to please me but especially, how to please herself, the uses for her cunt and her clit and her nipples and her mouth, even the simple act of stroking the back of her neck: that's what I wanted to do for Donna.

All of a sudden, I knew she was on her way back. I turned around and saw her practically limping. She had done it; she'd really done it. Until that moment, I hadn't been totally sure, hadn't trusted that she was a) curious enough to continue and b) able to get those cubes into her pussy. Cunts don't exactly welcome freezing cold objects, but hers had. She walked around me and sat down, a look of heaven and torture across her face.

"You're an asshole, you know," she said.

"Am I? Really?"

"I bet you're single. I bet all your girlfriends break up with you."

She was taunting me, teasing me, and despite knowing better, it worked. I reached between her legs, feeling the cubes threatening to pop out. She continued to try to badmouth me, but I knew she was just putting up a front. I knew from the way her hips lifted against my hand, the cold wetness alive against my fingers. I didn't even feel that sorry that I couldn't slide my way inside her just then. I could have, but I liked the tension between us, liked seeing her react, almost despite herself.

"I think it's time for a nap," I said, smiling at her wickedly as I took my wet fingers and brushed them against her cheek. My index finger roamed over her lips. She let me inside, only to bite me, and I gritted my teeth. There's nothing I love more than being bitten by a woman in the throes of ecstasy, when she hardly knows her own strength, and wouldn't care if she did. I could tell Donna was a biter. And a screamer. And a gusher. Don't ask me how; I just knew.

"Take it back," I said. "What you wrote before. Take it back and maybe I'll make you come." I could see *I don't need you to make me come,* flash across her mind, but she didn't say it.

"I guess you were right," she managed.

"You guess?" I asked, letting my hand rest against her neck, lightly, but with the promise of more.

"You were right, I see that now. This is exciting, it's not what I'd thought it would be."

"Neither are you, Donna," I said, and leaned down, pressing my lips against her forehead. Her skin was warm there, and I rested like that for a moment before telling her to reach down and fish out the cubes.

"What?"

"You heard me. I want them. I'm gonna eat them."

That seemed to be the most shocking thing I could've told her. I wanted to eat the melted ice cubes that were in her pussy. I would be tasting her by proxy, but she would have to touch herself to make it happen. "I'll guard you," I said, and shifted in such a way that she'd be hidden from full view. She didn't protest anymore, just reached down and shifted enough so that she could retrieve the cubes, which were about half the size they'd been earlier. Water streamed down her hand and onto both of us. "Put them in my mouth," I instructed her.

She did as commanded, our eyes meeting as her hand and the cubes entered my mouth. The truth was, I wanted to devour her: lick her all over, keep her naked in my apartment overnight, or, hell, for a week. But I let her fingers slip out, before taking them in my own and this time, settling a magazine across her lap and a blanket across mine, before delving into her panties with both our hands, mine atop hers. I steered her and guided her, letting her fingers show us both what felt good.

"I've never..."

"I know," I assured her. This was a hell of a place to start, and as fluffy white clouds raced by our window, I taught my own sexy wild child how to masturbate: how to make herself come, how to touch her pussy in a way that could transcend any number of bouts of bad sex or heartache. I stayed with her as she trembled, turning her face into my shoulder and leaning toward me.

She asked for my number, but I didn't give it to her. I didn't want to totally tame her wildness, and I figured this was like that "if you give a man a fish..." saying. I had taught her what her body was good for; now it was up to her to go out and use it. That's not to say it was easy to step off that plane and feel the culture shock of heading back to my real life, where wildness was certainly in abundance, but never paired with such innocence. I let her use my sweater to wrap around her waist, where a big puddle sill remained.

I hope Donna learned a good lesson that will make her a better lover, to herself and others, someday. I learned that you're never too old to learn new sex tricks, and that sometimes it's the least likely strangers, on a plane even, who can show you a new side of yourself.

BERMUDA TRIANGLE

Vanessa Vaughn

Justin arrived at the hangar first. No surprise, really. He was always the eager one. Before he had uttered so much as "good morning," he had his hands on my hips and had backed me up step by step until I was against the wall. As he held me there against the warm corrugated metal, kissing my neck, he asked if I wanted to go to our usual place.

He was a good student, the best. This was a boy who learned fast. He had grasped all the usual flight school lessons in the absolute minimum amount of time.

He was dressed in jeans today and a university T-shirt, good college sophomore that he was. He was a full head taller than I was. His hair was light brown, tinged with flecks of blond from the sun. I could see the smooth muscles of his tanned upper arms under his short sleeves. He held me firmly, looking down at my face.

"Not today. There's no time," I replied. "My other student will be here any minute." He was grinding against me lightly through his jeans. I could already feel myself getting wet.

"You scheduled someone else for the same time?" he asked, incredulous. "For today?"

"I'm sorry," I told him. "There was no way around it." That might not have been the truth, exactly. The scheduling hadn't been so unavoidable, but he would never know the difference. I shrugged.

I could sense some frustration in his stance as he stood there. He was hungry for me and cocky, full of youthful energy. I stared back at him firmly. In a slow, even tone I asked him my three usual questions.

"Do you want me?"

He nodded, grinning.

I ran a fingernail lightly up the front of his chest. "Do you trust me?" I said.

"Yes," he replied, as always, leaning a little closer.

"Are you going to do what I say?"

"Yes," he said simply.

I tilted my head. "Well, then today you're going to have to share your lesson. That's all there is to it."

Gently, he released my hips. With a sigh, he turned around to lean up against the wall next to me. He took out a pack of cigarettes from his hip pocket and shook them in my direction.

"Want one?" he asked.

"No. Are you crazy?"

He looked puzzled. I gestured around the building. "Jet fuel," I reminded him. God, he was adorable. I leaned in to offer him a kiss. He drank it in, hands reaching up to hold the sides of my face. I hooked my thumbs into the band of his jeans. For a moment, I considered pulling them off, just canceling the lesson right then and there and letting him take me against the wall exactly like this.

The squeaks of a heavy metal door opening at the other end of the hangar brought us back to ourselves. We broke away from one another, adjusting our clothes. We heard footsteps crossing the concrete floor. A figure finally rounded the nearest plane and faced us.

The first thing that always struck me about Eric was his eyes, and I was sure Justin was noticing the same thing. They were the lightest blue, almost a gray color. The effect was striking against those jet black eyelashes and dark hair.

I wondered if he knew he was beautiful. I had told him before, but I wondered if he knew it inside, if he radiated this sexiness deliberately. Eric always loved to be flattered. He loved to be teased. He endured whole lessons with me that were nothing but temptation, revealing more and more and more of my skin, until finally I would give him what he really came to learn. He was always the pupil, always eager to please.

"Am I on time?" he asked. "The professor went a little over today."

I assured him that he was.

I introduced the two of them, and they shook hands, chatting briefly about their majors and life at the university. All of their lessons so far at the flight school had been here on the ground. They each knew that today would be their first flight, but were surprised to learn that the other was in the same situation.

"So we're both new to this, then?" Eric asked.

I nodded. Justin gave me a look, wondering what I could be up to.

I clapped my hands together once. "Well," I said. "Looks like it's time we got on our way."

Preparations for the flight didn't take long, really. I talked them through everything. That day, I had reserved one of the largest single-engine Cessnas. It was a spacious four-seater. Most only had two.

I walked once around the plane with them, showing them what to check for. Eric ran his hand along its length as we strolled, caught up in the aesthetics of the machine, I guess; the clean lines. I only watched Eric, and smiled to myself as I caught Justin eyeing him too.

We grabbed three headsets off of the rack and headed to the plane with the keys. I tossed them to Eric. "You fly first," I insisted. He nodded, climbing into the pilot's seat. I took the copilot position beside him, with identical controls. Justin sat in one of the two rear seats. We put on our headsets and I motioned to Eric to start the plane.

It whirred to a start with an incredible noise, relaxing into a loud, mellow humming. The engine under us moved with the same sexy body-shaking vibration of a motorcycle, but at a higher pitch. It was a strange sensation because the headsets allowed us to feel the noise with our bodies more than we actually heard it.

I pointed out the appropriate dials and lights, going through the checklist with both of them. Justin crouched in the tight aisle between us, watching as we worked. At last we were ready. I signaled to Justin to have a seat and we all buckled ourselves in.

Takeoff was up to Eric, and he executed it perfectly. As we left the ground, he shot me a breathtaking smile from the pilot's seat, reminding me how much I wanted to have him again. I reached out and stroked him tenderly on the cheek. He touched my thigh briefly in a warm familiar gesture. I wondered what Justin would make of our little exchange, and glanced back at him. He raised an amused eyebrow and grinned. "Good," I thought. "At least no jealousy."

"All right," I explained through the headset, having to speak up a little to be heard over the noise. "Here's the plan. We're going to take a simple course. Just a long easy arc out over the ocean." I pulled out a chart, tracing some coordinates for them with my finger. "Should take about an hour give or take."

I corrected his course a couple of times, but could see he was getting the hang of it. He was quick to follow whatever instructions I gave. "Check your altimeter," I said gently. "We want to stay far above the water." We could all feel the motion as he pulled up. At that moment, I leaned over to kiss him. As always, I could feel the powerful passion behind it. I felt his tongue in my mouth, smooth but insistent. I loved the exhilarating feel of disorientation I felt in the pit of my stomach as the plane inclined.

"Hey, hey. Who's flying up there?" Justin interjected, giving Eric a playful nudge on the shoulder.

We pulled away from one another. I held Eric's eyes with mine and licked my lips. "Delicious," I purred. I turned to Justin then. Leaning into the aisle, I unbuckled my safety belt and kissed him. He kissed me back hard on the mouth, reaching up to knead my breast with his hand through my shirt. I moved away and settled back into my chair, collecting myself.

They both knew the questions. "Do you want me?" I asked.

"Yes," they both answered. From his expression, it was obvious Eric couldn't believe this was happening here, with someone else so close by. He looked cautiously into the backseat.

"Do you trust me?" I asked.

"Yes," replied Justin quietly. Eric looked from one to the other of us, a little confused. I held his chin with my hand, turning his face gently toward me. I repeated the question.

"Yes," he said.

"Are you going to do what I say?"

They both answered sincerely. "Yes."

"Good," I said. I gestured at the panel. "Flip that switch and give me control." He did.

"Now give each other a kiss," I said. I looked straight ahead as I said this, as if it was a minor, offhand demand. I gripped the controls, and waited for a response. I watched the small choppy waves passing far below us. For several agonizing moments, there was nothing. I heard no sound at all. They were either looking each other over, or sitting quietly on their own, stunned.

Finally, I heard the sound of a seat belt being unbuckled in the back as Justin crawled forward in the narrow aisle. I heard the same from the seat beside me. I looked toward them as Justin touched Eric's shoulder lightly and looked intently into his blue-gray eyes. Eric stared back, only glancing at me briefly for approval before Justin covered his mouth with his own.

I was startled by how different their kiss seemed. Everything seemed harder, rougher. They gripped one another's shoulders and made low mannish sounds. It seemed more forbidden and more full of emotion. They pulled each other closer, moving their muscled bodies together. I felt my clit pulse gently as I watched them. I shifted in my seat.

I looked down at the chart in my lap. I felt like we'd crossed some kind of meridian, finding ourselves in an unknown place. I thought of the maps from ancient sailing vessels, of uncharted territories marked with pictures of churning seas and tentacles and sleek scales, scratched with perfect penmanship by elaborate quills. But this wasn't new land we were charting. It was open sky, completely unreachable by everyone else. We could do as we pleased here. Now that they had kissed, we had completed the circle. This place wouldn't let us go, desire pulling us in closer like an abyss, a black hole. It was our own Bermuda Triangle and it had claimed the three of us.

After a few minutes, they stopped. They still clung to one another, breathing hard.

"Take off each other's shirts," I told them.

I heard the whisper of their hands as they fumbled against the fabric. First Justin's came off, and then Eric's was removed. Eric was still seated in the pilot's chair, Justin in the aisle between us. Their naked chests rose and fell as they panted. As I looked down, I could see that Justin was getting hard.

"Eric," I said. They both turned to look at me. I took a piece of heavy black fabric from my pocket. "Put on this blindfold." Without a word, he took it from my hand and brought it up to his eyes, tying it securely in the back.

"Now, Eric," I said. "Put your hands on the controls. I'm going to give you control of the airplane."

"But..." He began to protest, but I cut him off.

"You don't need to see. You only need to listen to my voice, and do everything I say. Do you understand?"

"Yes," he whispered. He put his hands on the controls.

"Good." I flipped the switch, allowing him to control the plane again. "Now unzip your pants. Pull them down." He did as I said, keeping one hand on the plane as he lowered his pants halfway down his thighs. He was hardening more each second.

I turned to the aisle and kissed Justin hard on the mouth. "Justin," I said. "I want to watch you blow him."

Justin smiled. I watched Eric's dick twitch with excitement as I said this. Slowly, Justin crouched near the pilot's seat. Beneath the blindfold, Eric allowed this stranger to position his mouth over his naked lap. I heard Eric's sharp intake of breath as Justin brought his lips to Eric's cock. He took it into his mouth, moving his lips slowly along the shaft. It was completely hard now.

I slipped my hands inside the waistband of my pants, testing my pussy. It was soaking. I almost ached I wanted it so badly. I watched the horizon tilt and felt a queasy but strangely pleasant feeling in my belly as the plane moved.

"Watch your pitch," I said. "Tilt down a little." He did as I said. "A little more. There. Perfect." He obeyed, now holding his hands perfectly still.

Justin was moving faster now, taking him in completely each time. He used one hand to tug gently on Eric's balls. The other he used to stroke the shaft with each movement of his mouth. Eric leaned his head back against the seat. I could see his Adam's apple move up and down with each intake of air. It looked strange and beautiful to me. I reached out and gripped the back of Justin's head as he moved it faster all the time. At the same time, I continued to push against my clit.

I could see that Eric was close to coming, so I gripped Justin's hair and eased him away. I checked several dials again and flipped control of the plane back to me.

"Eric, you can take your hands off the controls now." He did. He was eager to continue, every one of his senses heightened. "Get in the aisle," I said. "Kneel down next to me."

Eric shifted himself, moving into the aisle. Obediently, he knelt near me, his blindfolded face touching my armrest. Justin knelt behind him.

"Eric," I asked. "Are you going to do what I say?"

"Yes,"

"Do you want to come?"

"God, yes," he pleaded.

"Justin, fuck him," I said simply.

As soon as I said it, I heard Eric's sudden intake of breath. He was obviously nervous, but still so excited. Somehow, I enjoyed his fear and uncertainty. I looked into the back. Obviously, Justin enjoyed it too.

I saw the look of hunger on his face as he began to pull his pants down. His cock was huge and hard. It had been for a while. I reached back, handing him a condom which he quickly put on. As he did this, I removed a small bottle of lube from my pocket and passed it back. Justin rubbed some over his erection, stroking himself several times. Eric leaned forward against my chair, arching his back against Justin, trying to entice him.

"Is this what you want?" Justin asked, rubbing against him, teasing him.

I continued to touch myself, plunging my fingers in and out. My strokes were reaching a fevered pitch. "Just do it," I said.

At that, Justin pushed into him. He did this ever so slowly, and Eric froze in place. Eric was held. He was shocked. I was sure he was wondering how he could let this man do such a thing to him. Gently, I tilted his head back and gave him a long lingering kiss. I moved my tongue against his. I kissed his lips, his cheeks.

Because Eric did not protest after the first slow thrust, Justin firmly grabbed him by the hips and began to push harder. He closed his eyes as he did this, satisfying himself completely, plunging in over and over again, using him. Eric reached for his cock, jerking off as Justin fucked him. I glanced quickly at the horizon as I pushed into my pussy, curling my fingers forward. I thought of the rough perfect bodies beside me. I came hard and fast, surprising myself a little. I rocked with the force of the pulses I felt, feeling feverish and lightheaded.

The musty scent of sex filled the small cabin. I sat for a while, breathing quietly and listening to the noises the two of them made together. They sounded rough and primal, free of whatever niceties they reserved for me. They were free to lose themselves here. As I turned sleepily to watch them, I was complete. Eric's head was near my seat. I reached out to stroke his hair as he braced himself on all fours.

I imagined Eric's beautiful eyes shut tight behind his blindfold as he knelt there, enduring and savoring this experience at the same time. I knew just what it was like. Justin had done this to me before. I heard him grunting loudly as he forced his way in. His muscles worked relentlessly as he gripped Eric's hips.

I could tell that they were close to coming. Their breathing changed, their movements became more desperate and demanding. Suddenly, Justin pushed in hard, spearing him. The gesture was final and rough. As he shook, he pushed in twice more, then slumped over Eric's back, his breathing still fast. With that final deep push, Eric came as well. The sight of his come pumping over his fingers excited me even more.

Afterward, Justin pulled out, resting in the back. Eric removed his blindfold in a motion of pure exhaustion, resting his head against the pilot's seat. I slumped down in my chair, lazily piloting the plane. The three of us stayed like that for what seemed like ages, motionless and spent. We had no words.

I felt hypnotized as I watched the shapes of the waves passing below, light winking off of them. I thought again of those ancient maps, of ships lost in far-off uncharted seas, never to return. As I turned the plane a few more degrees, sunlight filled the cabin. I tossed the map to Justin in the backseat. "Let's find out if you can plot us a course home," I said, but I only half meant it. Part of me wanted to continue out over the warm ocean, trapped in our own lusty triangle.

TOP BANANA

Craig J. Sorensen

Big, bright yellow planes. Stewardesses dressed like shapely lemons.

What was it about Hughes Airwest that kept me coming back in those early days? I'd always hated the color yellow. Frequent-flyer miles weren't on the menu. Complimentary drinks and bad airline food were as far as it went.

Maybe it was that catchy jingle in their ad campaigns. Remember it? *Yes, Hughes Airwest flies more places in the west!*

Yes, yes, YES!

The cliché of the traveling salesman was in mid-morph: days on the road living in crummy motels out of the back of a nine-year-old 1962 Chevy, looking for that next sale. My cigar-chomping, bourbon-chugging mentor had just retired to a split-level ranch in The Dalles when I realized that life from the back of a car was not the life for me. Don't get me wrong. I loved the traveling part, loved the salesman part.

But this was the age of the jet-setter. Why schlep from town to town, selling commercial kitchen appliances, when the appliance of the new generation was just begging to be sold? No one understood these monoliths. They had flashy lights like Christmas on the side, and crate-loads of attendant gear to facilitate belching of green and white barred paper from a big printer that made the sound of a thousand knuckles cracking.

For a budding salesman gifted in the hard sell, computers were the stuff dreams were made of. How tough could it be?

The sun was setting as I mounted the stairs pressed to the fuselage of a big yellow plane on the tarmac of some nameless small city, bound for yet another. Truly, I had lost track. A handful of early successes had given way and my numbers were charting down. The sales of these big computers seemed to cycle hot and cold, and I was never at my best in the cold.

I was thinking of going back to selling commercial stoves, where grease-splattered diner owners knew the value of a quality stove, where my convincing presentations could amplify that value.

Tonight the seat of a Boeing 727 would again be my easy chair. I needed to clear my head. I needed a distraction. I'd sampled more than one Layover Lizzie: a stewardess stuck in a podunk city waiting for her next flight. I'd adapted my "fast read" sales pitch to sort out the women interested in such excursions. Make that pitch; if the client doesn't bite, move on.

This stewardess had fair skin and bright blonde hair framed in that damned yellow outfit. I didn't give her a second thought as I passed. But later, when she made the preflight check, her coquettish smile, painted burgundy beneath eye-matching electric blue eye shadow, lit up the cabin. I read her nameplate: *Jacqueline.*

Down the aisle some old curmudgeon pretended he didn't know how to buckle his seat belt. His grumbly voice let out a couple of laughs as she bent over to assist him. His hand sneaked around and pinched her shapely butt.

She gave a patronizing, tight laugh as she pushed his hand gently away.

I recalled when my mentor once winked at a beehived brunette barmaid somewhere in Wyoming. "I'd sure like to get into those panties."

She winked back. "Why's that, hon? There's already one asshole in there."

His smile fell like a luckless horseshoe.

When Jacqueline brought me a scotch, I tossed out my favorite icebreaker to Hughes Airwest stewardesses. "Is it true what they say in the commercials?"

"What is that, sir?"

"That you say 'yes.'"

"Well, we do our best."

I gave a sly wink.

She smiled softly.

The exploratory touch, the "innocent" graze of a passing knee with an innocent swoosh was met with a focused gaze that burned on my retinas like a sudden flashbulb on a dark night.

A few weeks later, Jacqueline greeted me warmly as she took my boarding pass. When she served my scotch, I tested the waters again. She hadn't said yes the last time, but I thought the moment worthy of another sales pitch. Casual, ever casual, the backs of my knuckles touched the base of her silky thigh while I "reached" under the seat for my leather valise. Her eyes connected with mine. They didn't squint, didn't widen. She let me linger for a moment before she eased her leg from my graze.

I was more deliberate in the dark cabin when she brought a refill. My fingers curled around the back of her knee to the base of her thigh. She watched the scotch pour. She finished as my fingers trailed up her thigh just under the bright yellow miniskirt.

I was sure I saw her wink in the dark cabin as she continued up the aisle. I pivoted my hard-on parallel with my pinstripes.

The plane descended toward a yawning sunrise. "Jacqueline, we should be arriving just in time for breakfast. I know a great diner just in town." I smiled as she paused to check my seat belt.

"I'm sorry, Mr. Gartner, but I have plans."

"I thought you Hughes Airwest employees say yes!" I gave a sly wink.

"Well, we do our best." Her lips curled in a tight smile.

Not long later, Jacqueline and I met yet again. It seemed fate had something in mind. She beamed as she took my boarding pass. "Good evening, Mr. Gartner." She didn't even look down at my ticket. She remembered my name!

"Please, Jacqueline, call me Kevin."

"Of course, Kevin. As you wish. If you should need anything, don't hesitate to call on me." Her smile gleamed like pearls.

It would be a four-hour flight, and from the diminutive turnout at the gate the plane was going to be sparsely populated. I stopped halfway to my seat and looked back at Jacqueline as she greeted another passenger. Her eyes were on me. I thought I might ask her to join me for breakfast, and maybe dinner "after," but the truth was I would be staying a good two hours from the airport in some town built around a large factory. The woman behind me tapped her foot impatiently at my blocking the aisle.

Jacqueline's smile widened. *Yes, yes, YES!*

This might be that moment when I'd finally join the Mile High Club.

Jacqueline sent a signal as she poured my scotch ever so slowly, a signal clear as the rarified air at thirty-five thousand feet. My knuckles slid from the arm of my seat to her knee. The scotch continued to trickle. I traced up under her skirt. The scotch stopped halfway through the pour. It was as if it was a beer and she was waiting for the head to settle.

I felt a tiny shock of curly hair. No panties! I eased one fingertip inside her as a light went up at a seat down the aisle. *Damn!* I withdrew my finger and traced her dew down her thigh.

I breathed her aroma as I sipped my scotch. Each time she passed me, she locked my gaze, and my cock got as hard as the fuselage of the 727. I drank my scotch a little faster than usual. The reading lights were shutting off all around the plane like the porchlights of a one-horse town after nine o'clock. Heavy, sleepy breaths began to rise in the darkened cabin.

I held up my empty little scotch bottle and shook it like a bell. Jacqueline returned with a fresh bottle. She set it on my tray and looked at me, waiting.

"Will you pour it, Jacqueline?"

"Of course." She opened the bottle and began pouring slowly. I slid my hand straight up to her pantyless pussy. She leaned close to my face, so close it could've been a kiss, and her Certs breath filled my nose. She whispered. "Go back to the bathroom on your left. Take off all your clothes and wait. I'll knock two times, pause, then two more. Unlock the door only for that knock. Any other, tell them you're sick and to go away."

It's hard to negotiate with a raging hard-on. I followed

her instructions to the letter. My heart jackhammered when two knocks came. The silence seemed an eternity. Two more knocks.

Jacqueline pinched her full lower lip tight in her teeth as I cracked the door. She nodded for me to open up. I cupped my hardness in my hand as she opened the door wide. She closed it, then gently spread my wrists and my cock pointed at her yellow-clad hip. She winked. "I'll give you credit. You do have a lot of nerve."

"Pardon?"

"You're almost too perfect." Her face was sweet and warm, but there was a darkness swelling in her eyes. "You've got a beautiful cock, though." She traced it.

"Uh, thank you?"

"Spread your legs."

I surveyed the tiny lavatory. She turned so the front of her yellow dress was pressed to my back like a chair. One cool hand smoothed down my back, across my butt, around my hip. The other circled my cock tightly. "Spread your legs," she repeated.

I opened my feet as far as I could.

"Wider."

I bowed my knees like a cowboy on a thick horse. Her hand slid under my asscrack. "What are you doing?"

She leaned in and whispered. "I was so glad when I saw you board the plane."

"Really?"

"Yes. You believe in karma?"

Truth was, I'd heard the lyrics in the John Lennon song, "Instant Karma." I had no fucking idea what it meant. "Yes, I believe in karma."

Her little laugh was hollow but sweet. "Me, too. I'm celebrating tonight."

"What are you celebrating?" My words became choppy and awkward as she gently squeezed my balls. My sac tightened.

"It's my last flight as a stewardess. I'd like to go out with a bang."

"Glad to be able to help."

"Of course. Say, you seem to know that Hughes Airwest jingle pretty well."

I grinned. "Yes."

"What is it they call us?"

"Top Banana in the West?"

"Mmm-hmm." Her finger slid back from my tight balls and pushed at my asshole.

"Wait, what are you—" Her finger popped inside. "Whoa!" A long banana had appeared on the sink. "I—"

Her finger descended to another knuckle and I gasped. I grabbed her bare arm and her free hand gripped my cock. She stroked slowly, deliciously. My arms fell slack.

"You're kinda cute, with your salesman pitch and smart-ass smile. You think you're entitled, don't you?" She stared, half anticipating my reply, half not caring.

I opened my mouth to protest, and gulped air. I squeaked as she popped her finger out.

"Admit it, Kevin. You feel entitled."

"Yes, I do."

"Good. Put your hands on your head." She kissed my cheek.

I complied. She pulled out a tube and started to squeeze it. A juicy dollop of clear fluid splattered her fingers. She reached around my back again and slathered the rim of my hole. I felt like I'd just plunged into a cold pool on a hot day. It felt weird, but that cool goo also felt very good.

"Who is Top Banana?" Her other hand gently cupped my tight balls.

"Unh!"

Her middle finger poked back in, and I almost came when she grabbed my cock like a handlebar. "Who is Top Banana?"

"Hughes Airwest?"

"Who?" Her finger pushed deeper while her other hand doused the long yellow fruit. Her slick finger popped out. She glazed the banana and it disappeared around my hip.

"You're Top Banana, ma'am."

"That's better." And the tip of the fruit kissed my sphincter.

It pushed in a little and my ass resisted. "Unh! Mmm!"

She pushed the banana just a little deeper.

"Jacqueline?"

"Shh."

My mouth gaped as she stroked my cock, then cradled my balls. "Ohh." The fruit descended a bit deeper. "Ma'am?"

"Shh."

With each twitch of resistance, she stopped until I relaxed, then she pushed a bit farther, holding my body fast with my hard-on. All the nerves in my asshole felt like they had been suddenly brought to life after a long coma. Each additional push made my limbs tingle.

"You like this, don't you?"

"No." But my rod was now dark purple, pointing at the vibrating ceiling, and the veins popped like the Rocky Mountains up from the plains.

She stopped. "No?" She tilted her head sweetly and began to ease the banana out.

"Oh, I do like it, ma'am. I like it a lot."

The banana moved deeper and it seemed like I would burst in a hail of ribbons. "Thought so." Her fingers slopped the copious fluid from my cock, which juiced like a pussy.

I felt the orgasm begin to grow in my groin.

"Not yet. I'm Top Banana, and you come when I say."

"Yes—mmm! Yes, ma'am."

She fucked my ass slowly, then she increased her speed. The sliding fruit was splitting me. Tendrils of ecstasy mingled with luxurious pain. She knew just when to fuck, just when to stop. She stroked me while turning the banana in me like a stick shift.

Not accustomed to waiting for release, I found the long journey excruciating and exciting. My hands remained obediently locked over my head.

There was a knock on the door.

"I unh—"

"You okay?" An elderly woman's sweet voice dripped with concern.

God! How long has it been? "Uh—" The banana pushed deeper. "Ohh. Just a little uh—sick—use—other—bathroom."

"Good boy," Jacqueline whispered. Her strokes, along with the pumping of the banana, widened and contracted like clapping fists. She bit my earlobe hard, sending a clear signal. *Keep quiet!* I fought to comply. The opposing pressure forced my first blast of come to explode so hard I heard it thump against the wall. She turned it like a machine gun and it shot short bursts across the sink, over the lowered toilet seat. I actually worried I wouldn't be able to stop coming.

As I drew breaths like a marathon runner after a race, Jacqueline scrubbed her hands. "Clean up this mess and get back to your seat. There may be turbulence ahead." She opened the little door and peered out, then was swallowed into the cabin.

When she returned to my seat with a complimentary scotch, she smiled softly and sweetly. I kept my hands neatly folded on my tray while she trickled the brown malt slowly, luxuriously over the ice.

She pressed her face close to mine and licked her lips. The bouquet of fresh Certs filled my nose in a whisper. “Who’s Top Banana?”

“You are, ma’am.”

“Good boy.”

My sales manager called me into his office. “Kevin, your sales have been tracking two-hundred percent above the average over the last few months. I admit that for a time I had doubts you’d make the transition to computer sales.”

“It did take a while to get my head around it.”

“Well, you did. I got a call back from one of your recent sales. He said the damnedest thing: ‘Kevin made the pain of spending so much on this equipment feel like a pleasure.’ Not sure what that means.”

I swallowed the urge to laugh.

“It’s no big deal. These computers sell themselves.” I took a big mouthful of coffee.

“No, no they don’t, and you know it. Really, though, you’re my youngest salesman, you really are top banana in my book.”

I spat my coffee down the side of his teak desk.

Of course, I cleaned it up thoroughly.

Brenda was a pretty, chestnut-haired, amber-eyed stewardess. She had a gentle smile on her lean, angular face as she brought me my first complimentary club soda on a red-eye flight to the Midwest.

Later, as she poured me a coffee, the lights in the cabin were switching off. She lingered nearby. “Brenda, will you join me for breakfast in St. Louis?”

“That’s very sweet, but I shouldn’t.”

“Really, just breakfast. I’d like to get to know you a little better, that’s all.”

"You see, Mr. Gartner—"

"Please, call me Kevin."

"Kevin. I never go out with passengers." I'd seen the blue-suited salesman four aisles up pinch her butt as she poured his third gin.

"Never?"

"Well, usually." She bit her lip.

"Maybe this once?"

She thought for a moment. "Frankly, we deal with so many, pardon my French, assholes." She looked four rows up the aisle. Her soft eyes gleamed darkly just for a magical second. "Sometimes I just want—well, anyway. I mean, you are different, you're a gentleman, but—"

"No need to explain. Maybe we'll meet again sometime under better circumstances."

Brenda paused. "I should know better, with that salesman's smile of yours." She didn't say it, but I heard *smart-ass salesman's smile.* I tried not to flash it.

She tilted her head slightly. "Yes, I'll join you for breakfast."

Bless her heart, Brenda married this smart-ass smiling salesman.

And to this day, from time to time, I come to the bedroom holding a nice long banana. Brenda's sweet eyes gleam dark and her smile stretches wide. She disappears into the walk-in closet while I go into the bathroom and strip. She knocks the secret knock on the bathroom door.

Clad in that bright yellow silk baby doll, she steps inside.

"Who is Top Banana?"

"You are, ma'am!"

NASTY LITTLE HABIT

Donna George Storey

Today's the day I'll break my nasty little habit once and for all.

That's what I tell myself as I shuffle on to the London-bound plane with the other Premiere Executives. I'm the only woman in the bunch, which isn't unusual. Before I decided to change my ways, the closeness of so many anonymous male bodies was the first thing to get me in the mood for later misbehavior. I'd imagine them gathered around me as I pleasured myself, cocks in hand, ready to shoot their loads all over me until every inch of my flesh glistened like a freshly glazed doughnut.

Today, however, I resolutely wipe such thoughts from my mind as I hurry through the business class cabin—no upgrade this time, alas—and silently repeat my vow.

I will not masturbate under the blanket on this flight.

I murmur it, under my breath, as I slip my suitcase into the overhead bin.

I will not masturbate under the blanket on this flight.

Pulling my book from my shoulder bag, I settle into seat 33B. Call me a masochist, but I specifically requested a center seat rather than my usual window. Breaking bad habits always requires a certain amount of discomfort, and it will be that much harder to jam my hand down my pants with a vigilant stranger on either side.

I pick up the plastic-wrapped blanket from my chair and push it under the seat in front of me, well out of temptation's way. It'll make for a chilly night, but I can hardly masturbate under the blanket if I have no blanket, can I?

"Excuse me."

It's a male voice, obviously the occupant of 33A. I don't even look his way as I rise and step into the aisle to let him pass. He gives me a nice "Thank you," but I continue to ignore him, except to notice that he's tall and sturdy, which means he'll probably hog the armrest.

My new row mate makes all the requisite motions of unpacking and buckling his seat belt, while I try my best to focus on my book. I can feel him glancing over at me, though, and it's all I can do not to roll my eyes. One vow I've had no trouble keeping is to reject overtures from chatty neighbors on long flights, especially men. I do enough coddling of male egos in my work. I've recently been promoted to VP of marketing, North America for a power tool company, and my coworkers and customers are virtually all men. Sometimes I need a break from the cordless screwdriver crowd.

My neighbor clears his throat softly, but with obvious intent.

He's certainly persistent. In spite of myself, I glance over, not at his face, but at his hands resting in his lap.

I do a double take. He's holding the very same book I have: the new paperback edition of *The View from Castle Rock*. A guy reading Alice Munro?

He says, "It looks like we have something in common."

I smile. "I didn't know men were allowed to read fiction by highbrow female Canadian authors."

"Oh, I'm not reading it. I just bought it for the pictures."

For the first time I really look at him: dark hair, warm brown eyes, and a smile to melt a glacier. He's not bad. Not bad at all.

"How'd you get turned on to Alice?" I'm actually curious to know the answer.

"I like her stories in the *New Yorker* and thought I'd check out her latest book. It's very good."

I narrow my eyes. "What other authors do you like?"

"Let's see, John Irving. T. C. Boyle. Vonnegut. Sometimes I venture into Don DeLillo."

"Good. Those are all Y-chromosome writers. With that talk of Alice Munro, I was thinking you might be a dyke undergoing testosterone therapy in preparation for the Operation."

He lifts his eyebrows. "I guess I'll take that as a compliment."

We laugh.

By the time they bring around dinner we're still talking. Paul tells me he's a project manager for an open source database company and travels a lot, like me. We have other things in common: crazy bosses, older sisters who just had surprisingly cute kids. He runs 5K races and so do I. Strangest of all, we both just discovered a slow-food bistro in Noe Valley that serves "priest's collar" pasta. Paul confesses that his Catholic childhood adds a certain kinky enjoyment to the dish. I agree and tell him about my great-aunt, Sister Loyola.

"Maybe we're twins separated at birth?" I haven't had anything to drink, but by movie time, I'm feeling tipsy.

"Don't take this the wrong way," Paul replies, "but I hope we're not."

His eyes flicker. Okay, so he wants to drill me with his power tool like all the rest. I have enjoyed the flirting, but sense it's best to cool things down before he makes any further moves. Letting guys pick me up on airplanes is a habit I gave up for good several years back.

"Well, Paul, it's been fun, but I'd better get some sleep now or I'll never get over jet lag."

"Of course, I should get some sleep, too." He reaches under the seat in front of him. "Hey, I seem to have an extra blanket—would you like one?"

My stomach tightens.

I will not masturbate under the blanket on this flight.

Still, it would look strange to refuse his offer, so I take the blanket and tuck it under my arms, leaving my hands exposed and out of mischief. To Paul's "Sweet dreams," I smile politely and turn my head toward the neighbor on my right, a silver-haired gentleman who's already snoozing under his sleep mask.

I close my eyes.

The dreams that await me are definitely not sweet.

So, what'll it be? Masturbate now and get it over with or futilely resist the inevitable for another half an hour and then do it?

I squeeze my eyes tighter. I made a vow. I'm too old for this. I'm a responsible executive. Playing with myself in public is a nasty habit and I have to stop.

Come on, you know that cute guy got you so worked up, you won't get a wink of sleep if you don't diddle yourself.

I curl my hands into chaste fists. I have to think of something—anything—besides sex. What about Alice Munro? A great writer, so controlled in her prose. *She'd* never masturbate on an airplane. Then again, her stories are always full of sexual yearning. I flash on a scene in her latest work about a young man who's troubled by the urge to stroke the velvety skin of his sister-in-law's birthmark. It was slightly perverse, but the idea made me a little warm and tingly inside.

Now I'm very warm and tingly.

In desperation, I turn back toward Paul, hoping some pleasant conversation might rescue me from my own troubling urges. Unfortunately, he's already asleep, his chest rising and falling rhythmically, his lips slightly parted. I study his face, the thick eyelashes and kissable mouth. His hand is even more appealing—he is indeed hogging the armrest—with long, sturdy fingers and a tracery of veins on the back that reminds me of a hard cock. My left arm prickles from the warmth of his body. We're close enough that we could be in bed together, dozing after a satisfying fuck.

I sigh and turn away. I fly often enough for business that it should be a bore, but airplane travel still arouses me in some primal way. The moment I arrive at an airport and get that first whiff of jet fuel on the breeze, my blood starts to race with the promise of adventure and escape. That pulse still throbs now, *down there*, between my legs.

My fingers twitch.

The throbbing quickens, fueled by the drone of the jet's engines.

All right, there's no use fighting it. I *am* going to masturbate under the blanket on this flight.

With careful nonchalance, I slide my hands under the blanket and rest them on my thighs. Over the years, my nasty little habit has evolved into a careful system to bring myself off with a minimal chance of exposure. I close my eyes and fantasize like hell while I squeeze my secret muscles, sometimes lingeringly slow, sometimes as quick as hummingbird wings. I do this until I get myself so hot it takes just a minute or two of direct stimulation to come. Then I lift my hands slightly and clasp my right wrist with my left hand, forming a tent that lets my pussy finger wiggle away unseen until I achieve the desired result. After that comes the extra bonus: sweet, untroubled sleep straight til breakfast.

I don't need to search far for my fantasy today. My lewd mind steals Paul's large, tanned hand and copies it three-fold, one for each breast, the third to rest over my mons like some avant-garde artist's vision of a fleshly bikini. On cue, the hands cupping my breasts begin to pleasure me, expertly tweaking and palming my nipples, which really do stiffen and rise under my shirt. Down below, the middle finger of Paul's extra hand slithers into my cleft to tease my clit with a soft, circling motion.

Meanwhile I work my cunt muscles—squeeze, release, squeeze, release—until I'm almost squirming in my seat. Before long, it's time to ease my hand under the elastic of my yoga pants and finish up the job.

As a final precaution, I take a quick peek at the old guy, who's snoring softly. Stealthily, I roll my head to check on my second companion.

Only to find myself staring straight into Paul's lovely—and wide-awake—brown eyes.

I freeze.

He smiles, with just a hint of mischief, and bends close to whisper, "I'd like to help, if I can."

I wince, as if someone's poured a glass of ice water between my legs. Of course, the only proper reply is a huffy "Whatever do you mean, sir?" But as he continues to gaze at me with that knowing look, the chill in my secret place melts back into a pulsing warmth. Paul's obviously guessed what I'm up to. And since I so brazenly borrowed his fantasy hands for my pleasure, why not see what the real one can do for me?

I nod, just once, but Paul needs no further encouragement. With admirable smoothness, he raises the armrest between us and slides his hand under my blanket. Flashing me one last bad-boy grin, he closes his eyes to assume a mask of innocent slumber. Except, under the blanket, his hand is massaging my leg in a most indecent way.

Instinctively, my knees ease open.

His fingers wander higher, to the crease of my thigh, which he strokes lightly through my pants.

I grit my teeth. The hot, tickling sensation radiates through my vulva and my cunt muscles contract deliciously.

The fingers shift to the right, circling my mons with a steady pressure. I rock my hips discreetly up into his hand. It's so forbidden and exciting, I probably could come this way, but suddenly I crave his touch on my naked flesh. I ease down my waistband and Paul takes his cue to burrow inside. His middle finger immediately finds my clit, which probably isn't too difficult, given how hard and swollen it gets when I'm this turned on.

He begins to strum.

Each stroke of his finger sends sparks sizzling through my pussy. My cheeks burn and I'm trying so hard not to moan, my ribs ache. I squeeze Paul's wrist to steady myself but—devilishly—he only quickens the pace. There's no turning back now, because I'm a slave to that jiggling finger. I'm a horny slut who wants it so bad, she'll let a stranger finger her twat on an airplane, yes, she'll let him rub her wet, swollen pussy until she comes, which is just what I'm doing right now, yes, I'm coming all over Paul's hand. I grit my teeth to hold back the scream rising from my belly, ricocheting through my body, as my ass jerks rhythmically into the cushion.

When I open my eyes, Paul's watching me, a faint smile playing at his lips.

I smile back. "Thanks."

"My pleasure."

He squeezes my hand sweetly before he retreats to his own blanket, and I'm considering ways I might safely return the favor when suddenly he stands. "Excuse me, I'll be right back."

I blink in confusion. Where's he going? To take a leak at a time like this? But I'm too befuddled by that rocketing orgasm to think clearly and before I know it, Paul's back beside me, giving my hand another squeeze. "And now I have to thank you."

"For what? I didn't get a chance to do anything."

"Believe me, you did. I think we're both going to sleep well now."

That's when I finally get it. Paul and I might not know each other well, but he's clearly on intimate terms with my nasty little habit.

So we *do* have something in common.

Breakfast could have been strained, but we're too busy talking for any awkward moments. Paul seems genuinely sorry I'm flying on to Frankfurt, and when they announce our descent into Heathrow, he pulls out a business card and writes a number on the back. "This is my personal cell number. I'll be back in San Francisco on the twelfth and I hope you'll consider giving me a call."

I slip the card in my purse with a noncommittal smile, but after he's gone I take it out again and hold it to my nose to see if I can catch the lingering scent of his hand on the paper.

Yes, it's my rule not to sleep with men I meet on airplanes, but I might make an exception for Paul. After all, he helped me keep my vow not to masturbate under the blanket—and every manager knows that delegating a task is not the same as doing it yourself. Besides, thanks to him, I've learned another valuable lesson as well.

Sometimes breaking a nasty habit can be very nice indeed.

URGENT MESSAGE

Rachel Kramer Bussel

The fact that I have to travel a lot for my job as a fashion photographer has always been a sore spot with my boyfriend, Brandon. He works the day shift at a French restaurant, and in many ways is more of a homebody than I am. I like a fast-paced lifestyle, which is why I moved to New York in the first place, but even though he thrives on the energy at the restaurant, he's happy to veg out in front of the TV or just explore the city. Still, we fell hard for each other and weren't going to split up simply because sometimes I have to hop on a plane. The chemistry between us was strong right from the beginning, and hasn't let up, so we've learned how to deal with my traveling with frequent phone calls and hours of hot sex when I return. We balance our nights out with ones cuddled in front of our fireplace (yes, we have one in our apartment), watching movies or having luxurious sex on our shag carpet.

When I have to go out of town, though, he practically sulks. Or at least he did until we devised a high-tech, ultramodern, yet perfectly dirty way of dealing with my absences. I had heard on the news that several airlines were now offering in-flight instant message and Internet services. What better way to keep in touch with my man than by sharing every X-rated thought I had, while on a plane filled with strangers?

Usually I try to fly first class, where I indulge in champagne and ice cream sundaes and generally pretend I'm on vacation, rather than heading off to work. But since I'd had to book a last-minute flight, I'd been stuck with the only seat left—a middle seat in coach. *Oh well, how bad could it be?* I thought.

If you've ever asked yourself that dangerously rhetorical question, you know the answer: very, very bad. I wound up stuck between a drooling older man and a fidgety teenager of indeterminate gender. Though I'd never cheat on Brandon, I'd at least have wished for some eye candy, a hunky man—or, hell, even a curvy, cleavage-baring woman—to keep the edges of my vision occupied. So I turned to what at first seemed like a last resort: I logged on to my computer. The teenager was listening to some very loud music and the old man was nodding off, often with his head collapsing onto my shoulder. As I waited for my laptop to load, I knew that at least I could get lost in the endless offerings of the Internet, which I often do even when I'm supposed to be retouching photos or replying to email. It offers endless distractions and can keep up with my ADD brain much better than even a juicy novel.

The prospect of going online was enough to make me forget about the cramped legroom—did I mention I'm five-eleven?—and lack of food service on a cross-country fight. I went on and immediately checked my email, then logged onto IM, hoping that even though this was a red-eye, one of my friends would be up. Well, one of them was—a very close, personal, sexy friend. There was Brandon, or rather, Randyboy69, as he so often was when he wasn't at work. We're an equal opportunity online addiction household.

Hey sexy, I typed, shifting in my seat as I pictured him wearing just a pair of gray cotton briefs as he watched the latest episode of "Entourage," probably with a beer, or perhaps a joint, in hand.

You stuck at the airport? he wrote back.

No. I'm stuck in the hell that is coach. I'm high. In the sky, that is, I typed.

What do you mean?

What do I mean? I'm in the air. On my flight. They have wireless now, at least, while it lasts.

Fancy schmancy.

Not so much. But you can help me pass the time. Take out your cock. Show it to me.

I didn't mean literally, even though he could have, via Skype. That vision might be a bit much to share with my seatmates, plus I wasn't sure I could handle the prospect of Brandon's powerful dick right in my face. But I wanted to picture it in all its hard, pounding deliciousness, while he pictured me in my seat, getting nice and wet, just for him. If I'd been in my car, I'd have been tempted to ditch my shoot, turn around, drive home, and jump his bones.

You're crazy, do you know that? And I'm not gonna show you my cock till you take your panties off. Get rid of them and shove them in the seat pocket in front of you. I dare you.

That was unfair. He knew I could never resist a dare, or an order, or even a mere naughty suggestion. That's just the effect he has on me, which means that since we've been together, I've wound up fucking him in all sorts of public places, and we've gotten caught twice—that I know about. I've had to slink out of men's bathroom stalls with my hair mussed after vigorous blow jobs, have had my cover nearly blown in the middle of an Alaska winter after a quickie in his parents' kitchen (the coast had seemed clear), and many more adventures I'd have been way too shy, or at least, wary, to take part in before him.

But Brandon brings out the dirty girl inside me, the girl my straight-*A*, choir and track team member former self could never have imagined. Even now, I retain so much of my good-girl polish, at least on the outside. Before Brandon, I dated guys who would never think of wanting a lady on the streets and a whore in the bedroom. "Whore" probably wasn't even in their vocabulary, whereas Brandon loved to taunt me with it, whispering it in my ear as I teetered on that perilous, wondrous brink of orgasm, knowing that the prospect of being a woman of the night would send me crashing over the edge.

Where are your panties, young lady? was blinking on my screen—in red. Next thing I knew, he'd be going to all caps.

Just a sec, I typed, feeling a rush of wetness soak said item of clothing.

My panties were already skimpy to begin with; I like to travel wearing my sexiest undies to remind me that while I may not have my man with me, I have something to look forward to when I go home. In fact, most of my plain-Jane, boring cotton panties have gone by the wayside in favor of silk, satin, lace, and mesh in a rainbow of colors. Brandon has made his mark all over my body, and in my dresser drawers.

I pondered how best to go about this. Removing my bra in the locker room in college without showing my tits was easier than this maneuver would be. I placed the laptop on the tray in front of me, then undid my seat belt, trying to be as silent as possible so as not to attract attention. I reached into the waistband of my skirt and pushed one edge of my panties down one hip, then did the same with the other.

I had to get them down far enough so that I could wiggle them the rest of the way with my legs. My face was hot, and surely blushing, as he continued to type away, the screen refreshing as I squirmed. *I wish I could see you slithering out of those panties, wish I could see between your legs to what they were covering. Even though I just tasted you this morning, baby, I miss you already. It's just not the same without you, but I'm trying.*

Tell me what you're doing. I have my panties halfway down my thighs, I typed back in a flash, grateful for all those years of temping that had gifted me with the ability to type one-hundred words per minute, or one-handed, if need be. I wiggled against the seat, shifting one leg and hip, then the other, as I felt my panties move slowly down my legs.

I've got my dick poking out of the waistband of my briefs. I can see the head straining. I wish you were here to lick it. Oh god. I'm getting out the lube now, the one you got us last time, at that store...the one that made you scream when I rubbed it all over you. Every word he typed brought back memories of us doing it in various places. I'd found the lube at a sex superstore in Austin on my last trip there, and it had come in at just under three ounces, which allowed me to carry it on the plane.

We'd had so much fun with it, we'd quickly gone through that tiny bottle, and had to order a supersized one online. The image he was painting of his cock had me breathing hard. I bit my lip, wishing I had something to put in my mouth. He was setting off every hot button of my oral fixation.

I pushed my panties farther down, my hands on top of them over my skirt, keeping my eyes glued to the screen, as if what I were doing wasn't completely deliberate. Maybe I could say I had an itch and was scratching it, if anyone noticed. I turned to my left, horrified suddenly when I realized my potential audience didn't just include the people on either side of me, but those in the rest of my row as well. Any of them could glance over and see me slipping my hot pink panties down my legs, over my feet, and into the pouch filled with flight safety instructions and the airline's magazine. It would be a gift to some lucky flight attendant or, if they did a lackluster job of cleaning, a future passenger. But I didn't care about that; I cared about obeying Brandon's order.

Well, Cindy? Are you done yet? I don't have all day. I mean, I'm almost ready to come all over you, and I don't want to ruin your pretty underwear.

That was a lie, because over the course of our relationship, we've ruined countless outfits, not to mention furniture. His come has splattered tabletops, stoves, kitchen tiles, bathtubs, and couches, not to mention every inch of my body. I've left wet spots in plenty of places that hotels would be horrified to know about (we do clean up after ourselves, as best we can, but it's an imperfect science). I never mind if I have to replace a bra or pair of panties if what I gain in return is an explosive orgasm. That seems like a fair trade to me.

Almost, I managed to type back. The excruciating frustration of not being able to hear his voice, not being able to even whisper his name, let alone run my fingers along my hardened nipples or stroke myself between my legs, was unbearable but also arousing. The furtiveness was part of the turn-on, a complete contrast to his freedom to do whatever he wanted. For a brief moment I wondered if he was going to take a photo of his cock and send it to me, which would leave me no choice but to hastily shut down my laptop and hope I didn't get reported to the airline authorities.

But Brandon didn't do that. He relied on describing his delicious dick to me in explosive detail. He told me exactly where his hand was, how hard he was stroking himself. His cockhead looked *red and ready to burst.* He could feel the come bubbling up. He wanted to taste my panties. Oh wait—he was going through our laundry and fishing out a dirty pair to approximate what he couldn't have. I was trying to read his text while inching my panties lower and lower. Finally they were poised at my skirt's edge. I felt them trapping my legs as I widened them just so. Sometimes I hold my panties around my legs when I masturbate, legs up in the air, elastic keeping me in place like some erotic exercise band. I like the way they feel pressing against my skin, the resistance they form as my muscles flex, sending me on my way to climax. Now I looked down below me, as if I were searching for a missing pen, whisked them off and into my hand in what had to be three seconds, and shoved them way down deep in the pocket in front of me, nestled against a barf bag and a magazine.

My heart was pounding, and I'm sure my juices were leaking onto my skirt. I didn't care anymore if they were visible. *I did it!* I typed, and I got the praise I'd been hoping for.

Very good. I like it when you listen to me, Cindy. I like it when you do whatever I ask you to. That means when you get home you're going to get a very special reward. A gold star, if you will. I knew exactly what that meant. That was our code word for the glittery gold butt plug he'd bought me when I got that rave review from the *Times*. I'm not one of those insatiable anal babes who need it up the ass all the time. Getting fucked there is reserved for special occasions, ones that involved sensual bubble baths, oysters hand-fed to me, and me spending a long time across his lap getting spanked and fingered and filled. He prepares my ass so lovingly for the invasion it's about to take, I practically melt around the plug. This happens maybe twice a year, and I never know when it will occur. It's another area where I cede control to Brandon, knowing that he knows just how to please me.

As I was drifting off into an anal sex daydream, the captain came on and said we were going to have to put away all electronic devices. I hadn't come yet, but I was in that preorgasmic state that is sometimes better than orgasm, where it feels like anything and everything could fill my cunt and I'd still crave more; where my pussy is almost in pain with need. It's what I like to think of as the female equivalent of blue balls. It was so delicious that I almost forgot about Brandon for a second. I looked at the screen to see he'd told me that he'd poured some lube into his palm and was moving his hand up and down, fast as can be.

He's let me watch him often enough that I knew exactly what he was doing now. Sometimes he ties me up, wrists bound with red rope behind my back, once in a while a ball gag shoved in my mouth, so I can't touch myself—or him—and I just observe as he slowly, teasingly, jerks himself off, until by the end his hand and cock are one body part, moving in perfect sync until he spatters me with his come.

I didn't type anything back, just brought the screen closer to me as he stopped typing and I knew he was coming. *Love you, will call soon,* I typed as I closed my computer and slipped it back into its case. I shut my eyes and settled a blanket over my lap, hoping nobody had seen me.

I learned two things on that trip: coach isn't so bad after all, if you know how to handle it, and there's more than one way to join the Mile High Club—you don't even have to be in the air to do it. I'm looking forward to my next trip, and I'm sure Brandon is, too.

OBEDIENT

Teresa Noelle Roberts

As she waited for the final leg of her flight home, Celia's cell phone chirped. One text message, three short words: *Are they in?*

Yes, Master. Her hands shook enough that she could hardly type. Or was it her brain shaking, distracted, already slipping into the erotic daze that Dan wanted to find her in when he picked her up at the airport?

Celia tightened her internal muscles to shift the SmartBalls—a one-piece silicon version of ben wa balls she'd slipped into her pussy just minutes ago in the public bathroom—and to bear down on her butt plug. Although it was her smallest, the butt plug already felt huge, and curiously conspicuous, as if everyone in the waiting area must know she had something stuffed into her ass.

And it was squirm-inducingly wonderful. It had been far too long since she'd filled her ass on Dan's command, and the small toy felt like an extension of him, like his fingers or his cock, transported to another state to suit his pleasure and her increasingly heated desire.

She couldn't feel the SmartBalls much, not yet, but long before the plane landed, they'd drive her insane with need.

And she'd do more to herself to make sure she was in an erotic frenzy, dripping and shameless, before the flight touched down and Dan took her home again—home to his ropes, his collar, and his collection of toys for pleasure and pain.

Home where Celia was a beloved slave, both pampered and restrained by her master, trained to obey in every way, although he made sure that, more often than not, obedience was rewarding. It might be frustrating and challenging sometimes, but it was ultimately rewarding—like now, stuffed with toys at his pleasure, ordered not to come, and awaiting a bumpy ride on a small commuter prop plane.

The phone chirped once more. Another text from Dan: *Did you remember everything else?*

Wet and full and embarrassed in a way that just made her more horny, she looked around as if her few fellow passengers could see the screen of her phone before she listed the pervertable objects in her purse.

Good girl, came the quick reply. *Love you and good luck.*

Love you, Master, she texted just before the little plane started boarding.

Small as the plane was, the flight wasn't full. Thank god. They'd be in the air just over an hour and during that time, Celia's orders would take her to the bathroom several times. At least this way she wouldn't end up standing on line too often.

She shifted in her seat as they taxied, enjoying the feeling of fullness, the stickiness from the lube she'd slathered on the toys, the slight discomfort that wasn't truly discomfort.

God, she'd needed this, needed this fullness and this pleasurable torment, needed to be under Dan's sexual command again, even indirectly.

Not that she'd had time to think much about sex during five long weeks of doing her only-child duty, helping her mother get back on her feet after a nasty car accident. She'd missed Dan every minute she was gone, missed his laugh and the safety of his arms, the comfort of knowing she was cared for and protected, the pleasure of serving him. But from the time of the first terrifying call about the accident, it was like someone had flipped her sex switch to *OFF*. She'd just been too worried and stressed to care.

Dan must have sensed that, because he'd held off on suggestive talk and raunchy emails and the small, naughty tasks he'd normally assign her when they had to be apart. Only in the last week, when her mom was almost herself again, though still limping, and was just waiting on the okay to drive again before sending Celia home, did her sexuality reawaken.

Somehow Dan knew before she told him, before she even really knew it herself, and started sending her emails and texts designed to keep her mind in the gutter.

Of course, being the sadistic bastard she knew and loved, he revved her up long-distance, but told her she wasn't allowed to come until she got home.

Complying had been curiously pleasurable. It was also frustrating, of course, but this opportunity to be a slave again, to focus on his orders and his pleasure, to obey without question (or at least without too much questioning—she was only human and damn it, sometimes a woman just wanted an orgasm or six!) was a relief after weeks of taking charge in a messy, nerve-straining situation, of dealing with a tangle of doctors and insurance providers and a wheelchair-bound mother who was addled on painkillers half the time and miserably cranky with pain the other half.

When she begged for permission to come, he made it clear that he had a purpose. "You need to remember what it feels like to obey," he'd said. "I've had to back off and let you do what you needed to do, and it's good to know you can still be that take-charge woman when you have to be. But at home, you have to be able to yield to my will, and this will help you ease back into it. Best I can do long-distance without making your mom wonder why you're calling me to ask what's for dinner."

And she'd clenched and melted and thanked him at the time.

When she was ready to leave, Dan sent a list of very explicit instructions for the flight home, instructions that would make sure she arrived home as a wet, yielding, obedient slut.

And again, she'd thanked him.

That was before she thought it through, though, and realized just how hard it would be; before she'd begun to follow his instructions.

Wet, she was managing just fine. The yielding and obedient part, though, was getting harder by the second. The toys were supposed to be a slow tease that built throughout the flight, but she was getting aroused too fast. She could clench a few times and come right now, in her seat, with no one the wiser.

Not even Dan.

And as the plane began to move, jouncing a bit on the runway and jouncing the toys that filled her, that sounded tempting. It had been so damn long.

Right now, she wasn't obeying because it was the right thing to do, or because she wanted to please him, but because the payoff would be worth the wait. One hands-free orgasm now would help take the edge off her frustration, but it wouldn't be anything like the amazing welcome-home kinky sex that he'd promised her in loving, explicit detail.

And she probably wouldn't get any if she screwed up now. She knew she'd confess to her failing—she'd never been able to keep a secret from him, even when it would have been in her best interest—and then Dan would punish her. This would mean his doing something like jerking off in front of her without giving her any pleasure, even the vicarious pleasure of touching him, until he relented days later because his own lust was getting the better of him.

That would be miserable, humiliating. And worse yet, it would make Dan just as miserable as it made her, so she'd have the torment of seeing his frustration on top of her own, and knowing it was her fault for being disobedient.

The plane took off with an abrupt force that pushed her back in her seat and sent tantalizing waves of pleasure from her ass and cunt through her body and for a tempting second she almost let herself fall.

She breathed deeply and touched the fine gold choker that was her public collar.

Soon it would be replaced by the stainless steel one that locked in place.

Soon she would be with Dan again, her love and her master.

She could be patient. She would be patient. She would honor him with the obedience he deserved.

But damn it, it wasn't going to be easy.

Especially when her body asserted itself every time the airplane bounced or jounced—and it was jouncing and bouncing like the clouds were a country back road laced with frost heaves and potholes. It would have to be stormy today, wouldn't it?

Finally, the FASTEN SEAT BELTS light went off. Carefully, holding the seats against sudden turbulence, Celia made her way to the bathroom.

First she used it for its intended purpose.

Then she used it as Dan wanted her to.

She pulled two plastic clothespins from her purse and tugged her sweater up.

Under the sweater's loose, casual cotton, she was braless—pantyless as well, which was usual when she was with Dan. For a few seconds, she looked at her bare breasts in the tiny, spotty mirror, trying to see them as Dan did. To her, they seemed merely average, but Dan loved them, loved to caress and praise them, loved to bruise them, loved to hurt them and then kiss them better again.

They'd be ready for kissing better by the time she got home, although she imagined there'd be more hurting first. Lucky her.

She grasped one nipple between thumb and forefinger, and stifled a gasp at how sensitive they already were.

Then she pinched the erect nubbin in the grasp of a green clothespin, repeating the procedure on the other side with a red one.

Pain radiated out from her abused nipples. No, not pain—it was hot and tortured and made her want to whimper and made her pussy and ass tighten on the toys that filled them, but it wasn't pain in the usual sense. Her nipples craved that feeling, had missed it for five weeks. Before long, her nipples would scream for relief, yet she'd drip moisture past the SmartBalls, and if anyone had offered to release her from the torment, she'd have begged to keep the clips on just a little longer.

Dan would remove them when she got home, or maybe when they got to the car. It would hurt like the devil by that time, hurt like someone had clamped her nipples in a vise and then set them on fire.

And if Dan let her, that pain would make her come.

Celia glanced in the mirror again, and this time she admired what she saw: breasts marked PROPERTY OF DAN. They were owned territory, his territory, and beautiful as a result.

Dan hadn't told her to run her thumbs over the sensitive tips that protruded from the clips, but he hadn't said she couldn't either.

The touch jolted through her entire body. She swayed, caught herself...and then realized it wasn't because she was lust-limp. The plane was pitching, caught in another patch of turbulence that made it hard to stand.

Once she staggered back to her seat, the damn turbulence made it hard to sit as well. Each bounce and swoop tugged at Celia's clipped nipples and shifted the balls just enough to arouse her further. Her skirt was damp and sticky beneath her, and her whole body felt as swollen and sensitive and flooded with pleasurably painful sensations as her ass and cunt and nipples.

She'd never make it at this rate.

She opened her book, hoping to distract herself, but the print danced on the page and she found she couldn't care who the serial killer was or whether the clever female FBI agent could catch him before he struck again. Maybe if the serial killer captured the agent and tied her up and started doing dangerous, sadistic (but disturbingly sexy) things to her, or if she turned out to like a good whipping to clear her head...

That would be bad. A plot twist like that would keep Celia's interest, but it would only make her hornier.

She shut the book and pulled out a glossy travel magazine she'd picked up at the airport for just such emergencies. Pictures were good. She could handle pictures and gushing articles about pricey vacations, although each jolt and bounce made it harder to care about hotels in Morocco or biking in Bordeaux.

After what seemed like hours to Celia's hungry body, they made it through the turbulence and the FASTEN SEAT BELTS light went off again.

She checked her watch. Time for the next task.

The bathroom seemed more cramped this time, darker, and the smell of disinfectant seemed more pungent than before—not the sort of place that made you think sexy thoughts.

That didn't matter.

She hiked up her skirt, sat on the tiny toilet, and touched herself.

She was drenched.

She pulled the balls partway out—despite the name, the toy was shaped more like a three-dimensional eight, two ovals with a short, flexible rod connecting them—and then reinserted them.

Ten times, counting under her breath, each more excruciating than the last as she shuddered with the effort not to come.

With slick fingers, she then circled her clit, backing off at the last second from three potential orgasms.

The last time, she bit her lower lip hard enough that she tasted blood. The taste of blood added to her arousal.

He'd see her swollen lip and ask her why, and she'd tell him why she'd bled for him. And he'd say, "Good girl," and bite the tender lip himself, and then fuck her mouth ruthlessly as a reward for her good behavior.

Jesus god, let this flight land on time!

This time, she couldn't even focus on the travel magazine's vistas of sunny resorts and snow-capped mountains, let alone follow the articles. All Celia could do was breathe deeply, as if she were doing yoga, and glance obsessively at her watch.

Finally the announcement came on: they'd be landing in fifteen minutes.

She had just enough time to hit the bathroom for more wonderful self-torture. Remembering Dan's instructions, envisioning Dan's face, she tapped the base of the butt plug until it resonated. She felt like a ringing bell, quivering and vibrating, especially when she stroked her clit at the same time, pretending Dan's hands and not her own were teasing her.

She could almost smell him, almost hear him chuckling affectionately at her ecstatic distress; could feel, even miles away, the love between them.

But even in her fantasy, he denied her orgasm. And gritting her teeth, worrying at her already tender lip, she obeyed.

Finally, trying to put herself into his hands even as she tortured herself, she put clothespins on her slick, swollen outer labia, one on each side of her dripping pussy. The first one made her wince, but it was a pleasurable wince. The second one just plain hurt, as though her overstimulated body couldn't take any more. Her whole pelvis ached with need and pain and her nipples felt like they might explode and when she tried to call upon her love for Dan to keep her going, keep her from taking out the toys, ripping off the clips, and either coming or not, but at least not suffering anymore, all she could find was resentment.

Resentment would do, though.

She'd be damned if she gave in and let that sadistic bastard win. (Granted, she loved him partly because he was a sadistic bastard, but logic didn't have much place right now.) She'd show him—and the best way to show him was by enduring what he must have meant to be an impossible challenge.

Someone pounded on the bathroom door. She pulled herself together and somehow made it back to her seat.

As she fought the building pain and arousal, Celia found herself whispering the Lord's Prayer under her breath. She wouldn't even call herself nominally Christian these days, but at times of stress the words learned in childhood would slip into her head and the rhythm, the old-fashioned familiarity, soothed her.

Then one phrase caught her: *Thy will be done, on earth as it is in heaven.*

And wasn't that what this was all about?—Dan's will, and her will to do Dan's will, not mindlessly but mind*fully*, choosing to hold out, to endure, to do what he wanted to bring them both pleasure in the end.

Thy will be done. The prayer narrowed to that one line, repeated over and over. She wasn't talking to God, she certainly wasn't thinking about God, and the part of her that remembered Sunday school and Easter services was appalled at the blasphemy, but in those words, repeated like a mantra, she found stillness, peace, strength.

The bouncing when the plane touched down bobbled her breasts and brought tears to her eyes, but Celia neither came nor cracked. Thy will be done. Obedience.

As soon as they were allowed, Celia pulled out her cell phone and called Dan. "I'm waiting for you, love," he said, his voice going straight to her tortured nipples, her swollen clit. "How did you manage?"

"I held out," she said, letting the pride ring in her voice even though she was whispering. "Didn't let go, even though I wanted to."

"The whole time? I'm impressed. I knew you'd try for me, but I wasn't sure you could do it. Were you able to handle the clips and the toys the whole time, my good, obedient slave?"

"Yes." Her voice cracked. His voice was undoing her, undoing all her efforts to keep focused and still, arousing her as if his tongue swirled over her tortured nipples, her hard, aching clit. "But please...talking to you is making it harder. I was doing all right until I heard your voice."

"Good girl." She could practically hear his grin. "Good, obedient girl. I'll reward you properly in a little while. But right now"—his voice dropped to a bedroom growl—"Come for me, slave."

As her fellow passengers grabbed bags and got ready to deplane, Celia sighed and smiled, clenched her pussy and bit her lip again.

She obeyed, and let a silent, powerful orgasm rip through her as the plane came to a halt at the terminal where her master awaited her.

His will—and hers—be done.

AISLE SEAT

Stan Kent

I'd decided to burn up all the frequent-flyer miles that I'd accumulated over the years of jetting here and there and splurge on a business class seat to Rome for a long weekend in the Eternal City. After some frustrating ordeals dealing with airline websites and operators protected from human contact by a maze of phone options, I was able to score a seat on an Alitalia 747 from Los Angeles to Rome. The only problem was that I couldn't get a window seat. I don't like aisle seats because it never fails that just after I've fallen asleep the person next to me decides to go to the bathroom, and even in the relative spaciousness of business class, it still disturbs my hard-fought-for slumber, and then there's no way I can get back to sleep. I wind up staying up all night reading or writing or watching some movies I really don't want to watch.

At check-in, I tried to negotiate a window seat but the plane was full, so I resigned myself to hoping that the person next to me wouldn't have a small bladder. I enjoyed several glasses of champagne in the lounge and another couple of welcoming drinks onboard as the plane filled up. I was feeling pretty happy and relaxed as the trickle of passengers slowed and the time of departure neared. I began to entertain the hope that the person destined to occupy what would have been my window seat was going to be a no-show, and I would enjoy a truly relaxed flight to begin my Roman holiday, when seconds before they shut the door, in she breezed.

"*Scusi*," she said as she slid between me and the seat in front of me, her crisp Chanel-suited pussy only a few inches from my face. "No problem," I responded, and I really meant it. She didn't smile, and I did my best not to stare at her shapely legs as she stepped over me. She looked like a young Sophia Loren; she could have easily passed for a Fellini diva, and looked well heeled enough to relish *La Dolce Vita*. I was going to introduce myself, but upon taking her seat, she turned her wide-brimmed black floppy hatted-head to the window and stared at the airport runway scene through dark, large glasses that obscured most of a very pretty but pale face.

I regarded her from behind the cover of the in-flight magazine, my eyes peering over the pages in what I hoped was not too obvious of a breathtaken stare. The suit was definitely Chanel or some other haute-couture house—black cashmere with large cream buttons. She had crossed her legs and the skirt had risen up her thigh. The stockings were black and silky, and I knew they were stockings because the darker band at the top was playing peekaboo with her hemline. Her shoes were patent black stilettos, the red soles giving away the fact that they were Louboutins. She was the kind of classy, sensuous beauty that Italy is famous for, and the kind for whom I was happy to give up my window seat.

The flight attendant took her coat and hat and stowed them

safely in the overhead bin. My window seat beauty said a soft and sexy "*Mille grazie*," took off her sunglasses, folded them up and placed them in her purse, made sure her seat belt was buckled and shook out her voluminous dark curls before looking again out the window as we taxied, took off, and began our flight to Rome. As we soared through cloud tops, I continued to read my in-flight magazine as a guise for looking sideways at her stocking-topped thighs. Surely she knew that the split of her skirt framed her upper thigh, which meant she unconsciously, or as I preferred to fantasize, quite deliberately, fed one of my basic voyeuristic passions: stocking tops and all the sensuous treats that they promise above while deliciously emphasizing the beautiful below. Stocking tops provide the continuity between the refined sexuality of the shoes and the raw sexuality of what lies between the thighs. It is for me a treat of immense pleasure to slide my hand from silky covered ankles to lace-trimmed thighs, crossing that Rubicon to the soft flesh that draws my hand up and around and between.

I may have pretended to be reading about the latest hotel to open in some exotic city but I was thinking about stocking tops and what they say about the woman who wears them routinely rather than just in the bedroom. As these libidinous musings taunted me, I kept reminding myself that despite my overactive imagination and the fantasies it conjured, I should not reach across the small divide of the seats and touch her inviting thigh, no matter how much she might have been consciously teasing me. I should not let my hands wander to her stocking tops.

I repeated this mantra over and over, all through dinner, no matter how much wine I had with my meal. Even though the foldout table and tablecloth obscured her black-stockinged legs, I knew they were there. It didn't help matters that her black lacy bra shone through the cream silk blouse she wore buttoned up tightly to her neck, promising that she was a lady who loved lingerie, and here I was, a man who lusted for ladies in lingerie. This could not be coincidence; it had to be the Erotic Fates that had us flying together to Rome in adjacent seats for the simple pleasures that two passing people might enjoy between destinations. Joining the Mile High Club with this lady would be a much better way to pass the flight than watching a movie, even a Fellini one, which Alitalia always seemed to feature.

As I regarded my traveling companion, I said a silent thank-you to those same Erotic Fates for my hectic schedule and lowly position in the Hollywood pecking order. Prior to my flight I'd been at a pitch meeting and it had run late thanks to me as a writer being the lowest priority on the producer's calendar. I barely had time to get my five-minute summary out and hear the "Thanks a lot. My assistant will call you if we're interested..." response before dashing to the airport. I'd had no time to change, just making it through Friday afternoon Hollywood to LAX rush-hour traffic with minutes to spare, and in those spare minutes I'd opted for champagne in the lounge rather than getting changed. As a consequence, rather than my usual travel uniform of comfortable sweats, I still had on my best pitch suit, which was a two-tone blue skinny Merc rock-star thing with a red shirt, black suede pointy ankle boots, and a skinny blue tie. If the beauty in the window seat could have been an Italian movie star, in my suit, with my hair suitably spiky and carefully unkempt, I could have been any one of several fashionable rock stars—a desirable commodity to many women and a good conversation starter at the least.

Even so, despite my posing she paid me no mind, and after a few ignored smiles I resigned myself to a platonic relationship. Dinner gave way to dessert and an after-dinner whisky as I retired to the comfort of my iPod and set it to cycle through

Stéphane Pompougnac's *Hôtel Costes* collection. Laid-back lounge music, a hectic day, and a bit too much to drink took its toll, and I felt my eyelids losing the battle with gravity. I hit the recline-all-the-way-to-a-flat-bed button and fell instantly asleep, looking forward to waking up just in time for the descent into Rome's Funicello airport and a morning espresso on the Via del Corso with the spirit of Fellini looking on.

At first blush I thought I was dreaming, or had fallen into an Alitalia Fellini film, but the dryness in my mouth and eyes was real, and I was awake enough to know that once again, the Erotic Fates had been kind. My *bella donna* was stepping over my fully reclined seat. She had straddled the seat but a little turbulence and the skyscraper Louboutins had made her teeter and put her arms on the headrest to steady herself and prevent her shapely body from falling on top of me. As my body sensed the disturbance and my eyes opened, I saw her skirt slide upward from her full-body stretch. Stocking tops became visible and gave way to pale white softness that lead to jet black lace covering her sex that had to match the bra I'd earlier admired through the cream silk of her blouse. I'd fallen asleep with my overhead light on and the crisp beam illuminated her lingerie-clad pussy with porn-flick precision.

The underwear was La Perla and underneath was a pearl of a pussy. I discerned small tufts of dark pubic hair pressed tight to the slight curve of her pubic mound, and the bulge of her labia strained against the smooth round of the panty's silky crotch. Our eyes met as my gaze went from the delta of her Venus to her face and her long black hair that draped down. It was a sexy sight that would not have been out of place between two well-fucked lovers. She looked like she liked it on top, and I particularly enjoyed the view from the bottom during such hot sex, especially the feel of a woman grinding her ass into my crotch like she's trying to stay on top of a bucking horse. What should I do? Close my eyes and pretend I really hadn't seen anything and let her recover her demure posture? Should I continue to stare? Should I reach up to steady her? Should my hand slide up her thigh and cup her pussy? Should I then slide my finger inside the elastic and bring her to orgasm? Should I pull her down on top of me? Should I—?

Pivoting on the leg that was anchored in the aisle, she swung her other leg over the seat in a move that told me she had studied ballet, yoga, and at least one or two martial arts. She shimmied her skirt down, smoothing the ruffled material. I enjoyed the reverse striptease, and expected her to march toward the bathrooms, and indeed, she took one step, but then she paused, reached down to my iPod earphones and pulled them from me, tossing them aside, as if she was insulted that I had been listening to music instead of paying attention to her. Then, leaving no mistake in her meaning, she unsnapped my seat belt. And then she marched toward the bathrooms. That's when my heart started beating again, only twice as fast as it ever had, perhaps to keep pace with the blood demand of my throbbing hardened cock.

Now there was no hesitation, no should-I-stay-or-should-I-go, Clash-like indecision. I stood up just in time to see her disappear into one of the bathrooms. I took a refreshing swig of water and popped in a breath mint from the complimentary business class vanity bag and followed her steps. There were two bathrooms, and both were signed vacant. I looked around. Everyone else was asleep. There were no flight attendants hovering, and despite the Homeland Security warnings not to congregate in the bathroom area, I swallowed the lump in my throat, straightened the lump in my trousers, and pushed open the bathroom door.

For one horrible moment I thought she was going to scream. She was sitting on the toilet. Her knees were together, her ankles apart. The La Perla underwear hovered around her ankles. She was peeing. I was going to make some excuse when she reached behind her and flushed. It was a loud roar that I felt for sure would wake the entire plane. She seemed shocked by the noise and giggled self-consciously as she stood and reached out toward me, her fingers curling back to beckon me in. As I neared her grip, she grabbed my tie in her fist and yanked me inside the relative spaciousness of the business class bathroom. In more ways than one, this could never have happened in economy class. She would have never traveled dressed like that in the cheap seats, and there's just too much traffic and the bathrooms are tiny and usually too well-used and stinky to make fucking that pleasurable. At least I was getting my frequent-flyer's worth out of my 120,000-miles ticket. I wasted no time in shutting and locking the door.

No words were spoken. No hands were washed. The La Perla underwear remained down at her ankles. Her Chanel skirt remained about her waist. Her hands went around my neck. Our lips met. She tasted of the same Alitalia-issued breath mints.

The first kiss was a frantic melding. Our tongues fought for dominance as if the plane was crashing and this was our last good-bye rather than our first hello. Her fingernails raked up and down my back. We struggled for balance, bouncing from the wall to the sink, until I had her pressed firmly against the wall. My hands slid up her thighs, enjoying in stereo the erotic journey I had previously fantasized about. From the lace band of the stockings, I trailed my middle fingers along the crest of her thighs, up to her waist, where I reversed direction and slid down the *V* of her crotch, where I cradled her pussy in my hands. I slid one hand around to grip her ass, pulling her into me, squeezing the silky-soft yet oh-so-firm flesh while the middle finger of my other hand slid back and forth along her pussy lips, feeling her moisture flow, coating my skin until it felt as much a part of her body as the clitoris I coaxed from its shroud. Under my probing and assertive touch, she moaned and her head lolled backward against the wall. I took advantage of the proffered skin and kissed her neck, nibbling at the perfumed flesh, feeling her moan through her throat. Her hands left my back and found my shoulders, where she pressed down, harder and harder, until it dawned on me that she wanted me to go down, down, down, and down, down, down I descended.

I slipped the sodden La Perla silk and lace thong over her ankles and her stiletto heels, and put the underwear in my pocket. I took her right leg and lifted it onto the toilet seat, opening her pussy for my mouth. I grabbed her ankles, and held her long legs apart as I leaned in and kissed her thighs from the stocking top up to the dripping bulge of her cunt as my hands enjoyed the feel of black silk-sheathed legs. At her cunt I did not linger, but flitted on to the other thigh and down to its waiting stocking top where I traveled my tongue inward as far as I could go, teasing, angling my head upward so that when my tongue ascended I met that tender space between ass and pussy. I flicked my tongue across the rosebud of her anus. She tensed her thighs and her hands gripped my spiky hair, pulling at the tufts as I directed my tongue back from her ass to leaf through the folds of her pussy. She liked that, muttering sexy Italian encouragements that were lost to me in the muffle of her thighs and my unfamiliarity with the language.

She pulled my head into her body by my hair, moving me around to achieve just the right touch of my tongue until she seemed to grow tired of that, and I felt my hair being tugged upward, and I trailed my tongue up and over her clit and up through her tufts of pubic hair and over her lower belly until I met the material of her skirt. She grabbed my tie and wrapped it around her hand and pulled me upward. Once again I was glad I'd kept my pitch suit and tie on because she was clearly used to leading men around by the tie, and luckily I fit the bill. Perhaps, just as I had a fetish for stockings and legs and shoes, so she might have a fetish for suits and ties, and if so, we were an ideal pair. I stood and our lips met as she kissed me. She licked at my skin, not shrinking from the taste of her juices on my face while fumbling with my belt and the snap of my trousers, eager to free my cock. I unbuttoned her blouse and pulled it open so that my hands could paw at her breasts, reaching inside the half-cups of her bra to squeeze the soft mounds of flesh, the hard nubs of her nipples pressing back into my skin in delectable contrast.

She took my cock in her hand and rubbed it across her sex, and then she paused in midstroke, rolling her fingers up and down my dick, looking at me with large brown eyes. As she touched my cock she shrugged her shoulders and made that quizzical and extremely cute yet condescending face that Italian women are expert at.

A condom! Of course! "*Mi scusi*," I blurted.

For one moment-spoiling moment I thought our fun was done for. I doubted that Alitalia gave out condoms with its vanity kit. I had several in my toiletries but they were in my carry-on bag above my seat. I really didn't want to make that trek in my agitated state, but it was clear that there would be no love without a glove, so I reached down to pull up my trousers and then I realized that I was as prepared as a troop of Eagle Scouts. In my wallet I kept an emergency ration slid carefully in the change compartment. I pulled it out and let my trousers down. My window seat companion smiled and gave a little applause, adding a truly sexy "*Magnifico*."

She took the condom and tore off the wrapper, rolling the sleeve down my shaft with amazing rapidity and dexterity. She put her arm around my neck and pulled me to her. We kissed, tongues darting, bodies squirming as we struggled for just the right angle. I lifted her slightly and eased her down onto my cock, letting gravity and the slight bumpiness of the flight settle her pussy around me. Our bodies locked together. We were in a perfect position for up-against-the-wall sex; her long legs were anchored by the Louboutins, one foot resting on the floor and the other foot on the toilet lid so that her sex was open and the perfect height for my enjoyment. My hands went to her neck and I held her face toward me and steady as my thrusts jolted us against the bathroom wall. I kissed her lips, and she bit at my tongue and lips, pulling away to arch her neck. I bent and kissed her neck, trailing kisses down to her breasts, arching my back as I fucked her, licking at her nipples.

Pausing in my thrusting because I did not want to come just yet, I used all the strength in my legs, thankful for the many leg presses I'd done in the gym over the last few years, and lifted her from the floor so that her clit was pressed with all her weight against my pubic bone. I flexed my calves and strained upward, pushing her fully off the ground, watching as the Louboutins dangled from her feet. It was a sexy sight, and a position of extreme stimulation for her, judging by the way she reciprocated in her moaning and moving. I grabbed her ass in my hands and rocked her body and rolled her around my cock to give her clit a maximum joyride. The curve of my upward-arching cock rubbed right across her G-spot. Her rhythmic motions became small shudders and then more violent tremors. I gripped her ass even harder, pulling her asscheeks aside, opening her cunt to me. One of the Louboutins fell to the floor, and she wrapped her stocking-covered leg around my legs and undulated her body as she came, milking my release from me with the clasp of her thighs rippling through to the velvety clench of her pussy.

We stifled our moans and groans by kissing, by inhaling each other's heaved breaths until we'd fucked our passions away, and silence ruled. My legs melted and we slid to the airplane bathroom floor.

We stared at each other for minutes, possibly longer. Time seemed to stand still as the 747 chased the sun. She reached out with her fingers and touched them to my lips. They tasted salty and musky, and I kissed them. She stood, and playing the Prince Charming, I slid the fallen Louboutin onto her Sinderella (yes, she deserved to have it spelled with an *S)* foot. I stood and she bent and kissed my softening cock, before straightening upward in her heels to meet my lips in a soft farewell and thanks-for-the-fuck kiss. Then she smoothed her skirt into place and buttoned her blouse. I reached into my pocket and pulled out her damp panties, offering them to her. She shook her head and curled my hands over them—a parting present to cherish more than any souvenir or passport stamp from my Roman holiday. She motioned me aside and washed her hands, arranged her hair and again motioned me to stay still as she opened the door and went back to 12G.

I stayed for a few minutes for decorum's sake and then returned to my seat. She had already covered herself with a blanket and was curled up facing the window, her back to me. I curled up likewise, and for once, after being disturbed by a window seat passenger going to the bathroom, I had no difficulty falling asleep.

We skipped breakfast since we slept late, being forced awake by the flight attendants before the 747 dipped toward Rome, then touched down and taxied. Several times I turned to say something, to smile, to ask for an email address or phone number, but she would always look away. It was clear we were to remain anonymous. Once the FASTEN SEAT BELTS sign went off she waited for me to stand and get my bag. I handed her her jacket and hat. She smiled and said, "*Mille grazie*."

"*Prego*," I replied, and as she walked ahead of me to leave the plane she waved and mouthed "*Ciao.*"

I followed her through the terminal, admiring her sensuous walk, the wiggle of her ass that I had so recently gripped in my fingers as we'd fucked at 37,000 feet. I rushed through passport control trying to keep pace with her. Our bags arrived almost at the same time. She had porters help her with several large suitcases, and outside of the terminal I watched her being escorted to a limousine.

She didn't look back.

I fingered her panties in my pocket. I took out my hand and pressed it to my face. I smelled her lust on my fingers. I blew the receding car a kiss.

Welcome to Rome. I had a feeling that in a café on the Via del Corso, the spirit of Fellini was laughing.

GAME IN THE SKY

Elizabeth Coldwell

Sam waited until the flight attendant had walked down the aisle, handing out boiled sweets prior to takeoff, before snapping the handcuffs around my wrists. I had been busy making sure the paperback I'd bought in the terminal was stowed in the seat pocket in front of me, and didn't register the metallic click until it was too late. When I looked down, I realized that I was effectively fastened to the armrest between me and Sam, preventing me from leaving my seat.

"What the hell do you think you're playing at?" I hissed, not wanting to raise my voice even though it was a night flight and the cabin was only half-full.

"You've been complaining for a while that we never do anything spontaneous or exciting anymore," he replied, casually draping his jacket over the armrest to hide my cuffed wrists from passersby. "And joining the Mile High Club in the toilets is a little too predictable, wouldn't you say? So I thought we'd play a little game instead."

The words "a little game" sent an unexpected jolt of pleasure through me. Sam was right. I had been complaining that our sex life was becoming predictable. This was due to the fact that for the last few months we had both been working such long hours that when we got to bed we rarely had the energy for anything more than a few sleepy caresses. And my husband's little games had always been fun. There had been the time we booked into a hotel and he had informed the staff that I was his secretary, before seducing me in the public bar. On another occasion, I had heard him calling me from the bedroom when I let myself into the house, and found him lying on the bed wearing nothing but swirls of whipped cream on his nipples and cock. The handcuffs that were around my wrists now had first been used on me in the bathroom. Sam had chained me to the shower rail and fucked me under the steamy spray. I had loved every one of these scenarios. They were simple, exciting stuff that had spiced things up when our sex life was in danger of getting boring, and I had assumed that was how our games were destined to remain. Until now.

"So what is this game, exactly?" I asked, starting to become intrigued despite myself.

"Well, you're a jewel thief who skipped bail and fled the country, and I'm the detective who's tracked you down and is taking you back to face justice. Hence the handcuffs. I want to make sure you can't go anywhere without my say-so."

I was impressed. Sam had clearly been thinking about this in some detail, and with his floppy dark hair, stubbled chin, and crow's feet at the corners of his eyes, he looked as though he could be the kind of world-weary detective who was prepared to dispense his own unique brand of justice.

"But what if I have to go to the bathroom?" I said.

"I told you, you don't go anywhere without my say-so. I could make you wait till we land. Or I could accompany you into the cubicle. But I might be a gentleman and decide not to watch." Sam grinned a feral, sexy grin that made my pussy tingle. "But that's not your immediate problem. You see, I know you've still got some of the jewelry from your last heist stashed away somewhere very secret, and I'm going to use this flight as an opportunity to find it."

I wanted to ask him what exactly he meant by that, but at that moment the plane began to thunder down the runway, accelerating off the tarmac and up into the sky. I've never been a nervous flyer, but at that moment I was strangely twitchy, anxious for the aircraft to pass through the low clouds and settle at its cruising height so the game could begin properly.

Sam, however, was prepared to wait until the attendants stopped fussing around before he made his move. He accepted a gin and tonic for each of us, but declined the chilled, plastic-wrapped cheese rolls that passed for catering on such a short flight. If the redhead serving us wondered why I made no move to reach for my own drink, or why I needed a straw with it, she said nothing. I had to admit it felt deliciously naughty to be sitting there, exchanging banal pleasantries with a woman who had no idea that my hands were restrained.

My husband placed the glass in front of me, and I bent my head low to take a sip through the straw. I had never dreamed that one day I would have my movements restricted in public, and I was dying to tell Sam just how excited I was by it. He ignored my efforts to engage him in conversation, and simply drank his gin and flipped through the in-flight magazine. Finally, he looked up from the article on the Dutch bulb fields he'd been studying as though it was the most fascinating thing he'd ever read, clearly amused by my growing impatience.

He glanced round at our fellow passengers. The few who were sitting near us were either reading or trying to doze. The empty glasses and sandwich wrappers had been cleared away and the flight attendants were more than likely busy in the galley. The plane was quiet apart from the low, constant whine of the engines and the rumbling snores of a man in the seat behind me. No one was paying us the slightest attention.

"So how does it feel to be a naughty little jewel thief?" he asked. "Enjoying being in captivity?"

I nodded in reply, feeling a little trickle of dampness in my knickers as I grasped just how aroused I was.

"Good, because it's time for me to look for those valuables you've been hiding away." My husband leaned closer. "You see, I had a tip-off that you like to store things you don't want anyone to find in your underwear."

I shivered. Surely he wasn't going to start searching around in my clothing for some nonexistent piece of jewelry? Not that I would be able to do anything about it if he did, of course.

I had my answer when Sam's hands closed around my breasts, squeezing gently. Even through my blouse and bra, I could feel his thumbs rubbing my nipples, stimulating them, and my breath caught in my throat. I loved it when Sam played with my tits in this way, but if I gave vent to my moan of pleasure, I was certain someone would be alerted to what we were doing.

"Nope, I can't feel anything," Sam said. "I suppose I'm just going to have to make my search a little more thorough." As he spoke, he briskly popped open the top few buttons of my blouse.

"Please, don't," I begged, unsure whether I was pleading on behalf of myself or the jewel thief in Sam's kinky game, who would have been just as embarrassed by the thought of being undressed in public as I was. My husband's big body was shielding mine from view, but if anyone had been looking at me directly they would have seen the exposed cups of my lacy white bra and my breasts heaving with undeniable excitement.

"Mm, what a luscious little hiding place," Sam murmured, as he began stroking my nipples again. They were hard now, and pushing against the fabric of my bra. I squirmed in my seat, eyes closed, thankful that Sam's jacket was preventing the handcuffs from rattling against the armrest. When he gave one of my aching buds a gentle pinch, I couldn't help groaning, more loudly than I would have liked.

"Is everything all right?" a deep voice enquired.

My eyes snapped open and I saw the male flight attendant, a tall, strapping blond with a cute Dutch accent who had given me a flirtatious wink as he'd welcomed me aboard the plane.

"Do you have a problem with chest pains, madam?" he asked. "Indigestion, perhaps?" His gaze flickered from my flushed face to my partially displayed breasts, and his expression suggested he knew exactly what my husband and I were doing.

"Oh, my wife isn't unwell," Sam replied, "but she was complaining that her bra was too tight. I wonder if you could unfasten it for her, help make her a little more comfortable."

"Certainly, sir. It's very important that we look after the needs of our customers."

I was stunned. I couldn't believe that my husband was offering me to another man in this way. But the relentless pulsing of my pussy told me that even as my mind was recoiling from the idea, my body was welcoming it.

The flight attendant bent over and snapped open the front fastening of my bra, baring my tits. "Is that better?" he asked courteously.

"I'm sure it is," Sam said, still speaking on my behalf, "but why don't you feel them to make sure?"

He needed no second invitation. His large, surprisingly soft hands clamped around my breasts, and began to play with them.

Before the flight, I would have been mortified if I had been told that I would find myself chained to my seat, half-naked, with a stranger openly fondling my body. Now, I no longer cared. It felt so good. I glanced over at Sam, anxious to see his reaction, and saw that he was staring avidly, enjoying what was being done to me. That impression was confirmed when I stole a peek at his crotch. It was a solid bulge beneath the zipper of his jeans. Until now, it had never occurred to me that Sam might be turned on by watching me with another man, but clearly he was.

Just as I was giving in fully to the sensation of being caressed in this way, the call light flicked on above a seat a couple of rows in front of us. The attendant glanced round, looking for someone else to take care of the problem, but his fellow attendants were nowhere to be seen. Reluctantly, he released his grip on my tits. "I'm sorry, I have to deal with that," he said. "But thank you, both of you. Enjoy the rest of your flight."

When he had gone, Sam asked, "So did you like that?"

"It was amazing," I told him, "but you've got to release my hands now. I really need to come."

"I don't think there's time for that," he replied. Over the public address system, the pilot was announcing that we were about to begin our descent into Schipol airport.

"But I *need*—" I was cut off in midwail by Sam's hand disappearing up my skirt. His fingers pushed aside the gusset of my panties and delved among the slick folds of my sex, finding my clit and beginning to rub. I writhed uninhibitedly in my seat. With everything that had been done to me since the plane had taken off, I knew it wouldn't take much to push me over the edge. For a moment, I wished our flight attendant friend was back with us, teasing my nipples while Sam worked so expertly on my pussy. I wished the woman in the row opposite would look up from her glossy magazine and see me, so close to coming, and envy me the thrill I was experiencing. Sam's finger made one last circuit of my clit and my pleasure crested, my thighs clamping hard around my husband's wrist as I came.

By the time the redheaded flight attendant came to check that our luggage was correctly stowed away and our tray tables were in the upright position, my clothing had been rearranged, my wrists released from the cuffs and only my slightly glazed expression might have given a clue as to what Sam and I had been doing.

Once we had cleared the baggage claim, we headed for the taxi stand, hand in hand. Sam had been right, I thought. His little game had been the perfect start to our holiday, and I realized I was truly blessed to have a husband with such a kinky imagination.

"I'll tell you what," he said, once we were settled in the back of the cab, "I can't wait to get to the hotel so I can fuck your brains out. But just to give you something to think about for the next few days, let me show you what you're going to be wearing on the flight home." He pulled a box out of one of the pockets of his flight bag, and gave me a brief glimpse inside. Staring back at me, nestled in pretty pink tissue paper, was a large, black, shiny butt plug.

WHEN YOUR GIRLFRIEND WEARS A VERY SHORT SKIRT

Thomas S. Roche

In my view, when your girlfriend wears a very short skirt, certain things are expected of you. It's not a matter of abstract morals, though without question it would be ungentlemanly to not properly see to her with great promptness when she goes to the trouble of displaying six inches of thigh above her knees.

But more importantly, it's a matter of domestic practicality: communication is important in any relationship, and failing to hear her messages will cause problems either immediately or down the road, or quite possibly both.

Then again, I'll be the first to admit that I might have an off-center view of the matter, since my girlfriend is Emily, who has clear expectations on most relationship issues. Let's just say that on any given day, certain things are expected of me regardless of whether Emily's wearing a lime green micromini and six-inch stilettos, or a grubby pair of sweatpants and a Cookie Monster T-shirt. Truth be told, those expectations vary more based on her whim than on what she's wearing, but when she wears certain things, she's sending a message. Her very short skirts, she'd made it quite clear on previous occasions, were not open to interpretation.

And in the case of a miniskirt worn on the occasion of our first long flight together—a red-eye, mind you—there was even less interpretation needed. But just in case I was still wondering, as we boarded, she made casual conversation.

"What color do you think my panties are?"

I already knew the answer, or intuited it—but I played along, mostly because I was so impressed that she'd been able to say it loud enough for me to hear, but in such a decidedly casual tone of voice that no one around would have picked it out of the babble of conversation all around us.

"Black," I said noncommittally, choosing her favorite color.

She shook her head with a smile.

"Leopard print," I said, remembering this one time at TGI Friday's....

"Nope," she said, and kissed me quickly on the lips. It was done casually, in a way no one around us would notice, especially if they hadn't already noticed her short skirt and unbelievable legs, which most of them had. But the casual kiss told volumes, since her lips went slack and soft against mine in the way that made my muscles tense.

"White." "Pink." "Blue." "Burgundy." "Forest green." "Tobacco." "Mauve." "Taupe." "Clear plastic." Each got a smiling head-shake as we crept closer to the ticket-taker, glad we'd checked our bags for the now-exorbitant fee rather than play the carry-on game that so resembles big-time wrestling. Each of us had just a small backpack, and Emily's was mostly stuffed with a big thermal blanket—she hated that airline acrylic, she said. "Orange." "Silver lamé." "Raw meat."

"Raw meat?" She screwed up her face. "Now you're just playing with me. You already know."

"I'm not playing with you," I said innocently, thinking hard about what was under that skirt. "Yet."

She gave me a self-satisfied look, as if pleased that she'd netted a guy who could carry on a filthy conversation like we were discussing the weather. We made it to the ticket-taker, got our bar codes scanned with a beep, and walked down the gangway; Emily in front, me following behind, eyes on her perfect ass in that short skirt, knowing what was underneath but wanting very badly to check, just in case.

When your girlfriend wears a very short skirt, certain things are expected of you. If your girlfriend is Emily, that is. And speaking for myself, there are far worse things to spend eight-plus hours doing than fulfilling them—no matter what the in-flight movie.

The Boeing 757 is a marvelous airplane, and online reservations are a pervert's godsend. Emily had obviously been planning ahead, as she'd gotten us seated in the plane's exit row, which only had two seats. The arm between us pivoted easily out of the way; the tray tables were those crappy side-loaders, but it was a damn sight better than trying not to disturb some innocent third party. The first thing I did was reach for the blanket; she swatted my hand away and said, "Jeez, don't you even buy a girl a drink first?" She brought my hand to her mouth and licked my wrist gently, as if to convince me it made sense to wait. "Besides, I like it with the lights out," she said softly.

I pouted and paged through a plastic-sleeved *Popular Mechanics* while she paged through *Newsweek*. The plane powered up, taxied, sped down the runway, tilted, rose, shuddered all over and gradually smoothed out.

"We have to wait until the lights go down," Emily said

insistently when I leaned closer and my hands began to wander. "Then give it fifteen minutes. That's how you avoid getting caught."

"You've done this before?" I said.

"No," she told me. "I just read the FAQ."

God bless the information age.

"I'm not giving it fifteen minutes," I said.

"Wow," she answered with a merciless smile. "Tough talk, but I like it. How long are you going to wait?"

"I'm not. When those lights go out, you're mine."

"I see. You're going to find out what color my underwear is?"

"If I can see it in the dark," I said.

"Oh, you most certainly can," she sighed. "Then what are you going to do to me?"

"Wait and find out," I said.

Though I never, ever drink on planes—dehydration, you understand—I ordered a bourbon, and Emily a vodka. We sipped them while I waited on pins and needles for the lights to go out. Meanwhile, Emily casually got out the blanket, a soft full-size thermal; it had been the spare blanket tossed over the back of her couch for as long as I'd been dating her, and had seen more filthy goings-on than the barkeep in a brothel. She looked at me innocently as she unfastened her seat belt and draped the blanket over her body, omitting me entirely. "Do you want some?" she asked, eyes wide.

I growled at her softly, and she lifted one edge of the blanket. I undid my own seat belt and she let me slide closer under the blanket with her. She caught my wrist at her knee, and looked me in the eyes, smoldering.

"Not yet," she whispered. "The lights."

Several long minutes passed while the plane shuddered and swayed. Emily and I looked into each other's eyes like poker players trying to read hearts and clubs, jacks and aces. At one point she laughed, a cruel little giggle that told me how much she enjoyed making me wait.

Then everything went black.

All it took was, "We have now dimmed the cabin lights," and I was on her.

I pressed my lips to hers and tasted her tongue; she let out a little whimpering sigh as she relaxed into the seat and spread her legs a little. I made her wait, though—the way she'd made me wait, only this time it was simple torture, not propriety.

Our tongues tangled and my hand crept to her breasts under the blanket; her nipples were soft despite the air-conditioned chill, but they responded instantly to my touch as I eased my hand down the V-neck shirt. She whimpered softly as I pinched first one nipple, than the other, kissing her the whole while. A quick glance around told me no one was watching; it was sufficiently dark that I felt safe. Whether Emily felt safe was mostly immaterial, since she's always thought safety is overrated, and her "fifteen minute" rule was nothing more than a ploy. Turning back to her, I slid my hand up under her shirt and began caressing her breasts through the thin fabric of her bra. *Who wears a bra on a red-eye*? I found myself thinking in that strange way that practical, unsexy thoughts can intrude on a perfectly erotic moment—but in this case, I knew Emily'd worn a bra because not to do so would look bizarrely conspicuous with such a short skirt. Propriety? No, she got off on the game of seeming just barely respectable.

I eased the lacy fabric out of the way and caressed her stiffening nipples with my fingers and thumb, my other hand tucked into the small of her back and pulling her close. She clutched the satin binding with one hand and with her other, she reached out and began stroking my cock. It was mostly hard already, tenting my cotton cargo pants, and it got harder as she rubbed it. Her fingers worked at my belt, but she never got it all the way undone, because once I had her nipples ripe and excited I moved my hand down to her thighs, which were parted more than enough under the blanket to give me easy access, and I didn't need my eyes to see what color underwear she was wearing. She wasn't wearing any, which was the answer to her trick question I'd guessed immediately. But little games like that are the stuff of flirtation for Emily, as evidenced by how incredibly fucking wet she was when I began to caress her smooth cunt. My fingers went into her two at a time, middle and index, middle and ring, then three—middle and index and ring, thumb working her clit while she clutched herself close and hard to me, biting my neck and uttering dirty things into my ear. Her warm breath carried soft blasphemies as I began to finger her, feeling her G-spot swelling against the pads of my fingers, her clit hardening against my thumb.

"Shhhhhh," I whispered to her. "Don't make a sound or they'll turn this plane around."

She had to bite her lip not to make noise. She continued clutching after my pants, but didn't make much ground; to undo them was a fairly complex task at that angle, and she was intensely distracted. She got as far as my belt and then couldn't find the button. I took a moment from fucking her and lifted my fingers to her mouth; she obediently licked them and I kissed her, tasting sharp musk as I brought my wet hand down and quickly undid my pants under the blanket. I guided her hand onto my cock; I didn't need to guide it, really, but it felt good to press it insistently onto me. Emily's fingers circled my hard cock and began stroking up and down while she kissed me.

I took that moment to reach up and turn on both air vents, creating a loud hissing sound. We'd need it, I knew, because my hand's next stop was my thigh pocket.

It took Emily a moment to realize what was happening. The vibrator was silent, so she didn't quite get it until after the sensations began to flow into her clit. It was an infinitesimal, exorbitantly priced model I'd picked up at the local connoisseur's shop, which promised to be virtually silent and intensely powerful. She continued her hand job with one hand while her other hand lay soft against her thigh, fingers splayed.

Her body went tight and then shuddered all over as she realized she was going to come. I tucked the vibe between my thumb and her clit so I could slide my fingers back into her. I kissed her deeply as her strokes got shaky on my cock—she was close, and the three fingers inside her sent her right over the edge. She clutched me tight and buried her face in my neck, desperately fighting to not make a sound—and she succeeded, but just barely. I felt her pussy tightening hard around my fingers as she climaxed, then a series of frantic shivers went through her body as pleasure subsumed her. I switched the vibrator off when the spasms began to dissipate. Emily let out a long, low sigh of satisfaction, and I chuckled.

She was the one to surprise me, then, as she went down under the blanket and took my cock in her mouth. Her lips glided up and down my shaft; I glanced around nervously, but everyone was sleeping or otherwise occupied. That wouldn't last, but it didn't need to—Emily's skilled hand had brought me close, and her seething tongue and wet lips working up and down on my cock made me grit my teeth and let go. She milked me with her hand around my shaft and her throat muscles worked, swallowing.

When she came up from under the blanket she was red-faced and her hair was a mess, but we were lucky—darkness and the hissing sound from the air vents had covered our indiscretion. Emily quickly zipped me up and I pulled down her skirt. I went to put the vibrator away. She caught my hand and inspected the tiny bullet-shaped device, nodding her approval.

"You're the perfect boyfriend," she teased me with a smile. She took the vibrator out of my hand, tucked it into her waistband, and slipped out from under the blanket.

She kissed me once, her mouth tasting like the juices that covered my fingers. She climbed over me and headed for the bathroom. There was no line.

When your girlfriend wears a very short skirt, you see, certain things are expected of you, by my way of thinking. This being our first red-eye together, I'd surmised Emily's planned outfit, along with her expectations, and packed for the trip.

I looked over my shoulder. The plane shuddered all over, and Emily swayed on her way to the head. She looked back at me, pouted, and patted her waistband. She went in.

I waited five minutes and followed her.

PLANES, TRAINS, AND BANANA-SEAT BICYCLES

Alison Tyler

"You take a jet plane to a little plane. A six-seater, you know?"

Sasha was the one who bought us tickets to the retreat.

"The six-seater lands at this tiny little airport in the middle of nowhere."

"How tiny?" I asked, trying to wrap my mind around the location—did she mean tiny like LaGuardia compared to JFK or tiny like Oakland compared to SFO, or…?

"Trust me, Jaz. It's tiny. Tiny like no place you've ever been before, which is why this is the perfect present for you." My sister looked so smug as she said that, her frizzy ash blonde hair pulled back in a loose bun, her shapeless hemp shirt hiding the curves of her body. Sasha always dresses in clothes that emphasize the fact that she doesn't give a shit about clothes. Even though she and her husband Jarred are wealthy, they put a lot of effort into pretending that they aren't. I say *pretending* because Sasha's brand-new beige Land Rover was parked outside the café, and I knew for a fact that her ugly, no-animal-was-harmed-to-make-these shoes had cost well over four hundred dollars.

"A scooter is waiting for you by the airstrip. You know, one of those Vespas, the old-fashioned kind. You drive the scooter to a boat. Paddle the boat to a bike. Wind your way along a twisting dirt road to the cabin."

"Cabin," I repeated, dully. I could see the cabin in my mind: wood walls, no screens, the scent of pine needles and Off in the air. At least, I could see the cabin until Sasha said, "Well, tent really. I *call* it a cabin, but there's not a roof or windows, exactly. No running water. No electricity." She sighed deeply. "It will be good for you to get out of the city. Trust me, Jaz. It's so romantic."

Sasha pushed the envelope across the table. This was my older sister's big gift for Adrien's and my ten-year anniversary, and all I wanted to do was rip the tickets to tiny shreds and pretend she'd never invited me to lunch at all. I *like* the city. I like sprawling in bed on weekend mornings and watching the airplanes take off over the bay, imagining the people inside heading off to faraway, exotic locations.

But I didn't so much like the thought of what Sasha had described.

"You take a jet to a six-seater," I told Adrien that night. "Then a scooter to a boat to a bike to..."

"...A bed, I hope," he interrupted.

"Sasha said there wasn't any bed. Just a mat on the floor."

I hoped the horror wasn't visible on my face. I own a mat, for yoga at the center down the street. I'd never think of sleeping on one. But I was trying not to color the situation for Adrien. If he wanted to go on this impromptu trip, taking a vacation that we could never dream of affording ourselves, then who was I to be a killjoy? Besides, Adrien is adept at playing in the wilderness. He rock climbs on the weekends, fly-fishes in the summer, and he's been known to make fun of my lack of outdoorsy skills, teasing me for wearing high-heeled mules to a three-mile hike at the beach or bringing a flat-iron that plugs into our car's cigarette lighter to kill the frizz in my hair when we've dined at Half Moon Bay.

So I was thrilled when he said, "We have a bed right here," and tied me to the wrought-iron railing, my wrists over my head, my body naked, hot and wet and ready for him. The fans blew a mechanical breeze over us, and I drew in big gulps of the cool air as Adrien kissed his way down my body. He held on to my waist as he nuzzled the tender skin of my inner thighs, licked me right on the indents of my hips, those ticklish spots, before bringing his mouth to my pussy and suckling my clit. I couldn't think for a minute, couldn't worry about this vacation that I emphatically did not want to take.

"Don't we have a perfectly good bed?" Adrien murmured when he stopped for a breath.

I think I nodded. I might have moaned. All thoughts of air travel were replaced by the journey to orgasm as Adrien began to make those looping circles that I love best, love most of all when he has me bound so that I cannot fight. I have to give in. Who'd fight against pleasure like this? Not me. Not really. But being forced to take the endless rotations of his tongue, of his fingers, being fixed in place while he has his way with me: that nearly makes me see stars.

Which reminded me...

"Sasha says there aren't any lights anywhere. Nothing but the moon and the stars."

"Really?" Adrien asked, slipping back up my body to reach for something in our toy drawer. Quickly, he placed a blindfold over my eyes and fastened the strap under my smooth, flat-ironed hair. "With a blindfold on, doesn't matter if there are lights or not."

Oh, god, he was right. Who cared if there were lights? Who cared if we had one of those power outages that often happens when the city gets too darn hot for its own good? No, that's not the same as living in the wilderness, but it's about as close to camping as I ever get.

In this manufactured darkness, I kept up my monologue. Sasha had not only put the idea in my head—she'd given me the gift of a five-thousand-dollar vacation. Guilt had me nearly as giddy as Adrien's tongue.

"Sasha said that the nights were so still you can hear yourself breathing."

"I hear myself breathing all the time," Adrien said, bending down to me, letting me lift my head to press my ear to his broad chest. The steady rise and fall of his breath soothed me, as much as the sound of traffic outside our window.

Would I be able to handle no sound at all?

Adrien pumped himself over my body, and even with the blindfold on, I could visualize what he looked like: long dark hair pushed off his forehead, dark blue eyes focused intently on my own face, watching for the changes in my expressions that would let him know I was getting closer. His cock dipped between the lips of my pussy, and I could feel how wet I was. He thrust in again, slim hips meeting my body, and then he rotated slowly, so that his cock stirred me up inside. Finally, I gave up playing little-miss-travelogue. Fucking Adrien always takes me away—as neatly as a jet slicing through the dark velvet sky. I couldn't speak when he worked me like that: on a bed, in the middle of the night, with the hot air around us and the lullaby of traffic out our window.

But that made me think of one more selling point: "You're all by yourself," Sasha had said. "You and Adrien would be the only people there. Your own private oasis. Your own private island."

Adrien undid the bindings on my wrists and slid the blindfold from my face. I hadn't come yet. Neither had he. I felt as if I might melt in the heat; melt from desire, from the way he was watching me. Somehow, I didn't realize his plan until he pushed up the window and dragged me out onto our fire escape. I was naked, and I gripped on to the cool metal and looked down at the San Francisco traffic as he positioned himself behind me. His body was warm and strong, and he held my hips and drove in, hard.

No noise, Sasha said. *No people. No lights. No sound.*

But fuck me, I like the noise.

And I found myself adding to the cacophony as Adrien rocked his cock in to the hilt. I couldn't keep myself quiet as he wet his cock with my own juices, then slipped the head between the cheeks of my ass, pressed there—ready, waiting.

I groaned and lowered my head to my chest, desperate to climax. Adrien ran one hand down the front of my body, as his cock pushed into my ass. His fingers landed naturally on my clit, rubbing, rubbing to get me over the edge, to loosen me up to the pain-pleasure of the throb of his cock. His fingers became my metronome, ticking, tickling, so that he managed to time my climax with his own.

If we were all by ourselves, then we couldn't be exhibitionists, could we?

If we were all alone, then just like that tagline for *Alien*, nobody would be able to hear me scream.

Adrien shepherded me back inside the apartment, pulling me

after him to our shower. "No running water," Sasha had said. "You don't mind after a day or so. You get used to it." Even under the spray of our shower, we could hear the rush of the traffic rumbling by. When we turned off the shower and walked into the living room, air-drying in the heat, we could hear more sounds: a low bluesy number from our neighbor's stereo, the *tap-tap* of the leaky faucet in the kitchen.

"So how do you get there?" he asked, really focusing on the concept for the first time. I watched him lift the envelope from the coffee table—the crisp manila one that held the tickets.

"A big plane to a little plane," I said hopelessly. "A little plane to a scooter to a boat to a bike."

When was the last time I'd been on a bike? Not a stationary bike at the gym, but a real live cycle? I remembered mine from elementary school—outfitted with a banana seat and fancy high handlebars. Little fluttery streamers were attached to the ends of the bars, and they flapped in the breeze. The body of the bike was purple spangled. I didn't think that's what would be waiting for us at the other side of the river.

"Do you want to go?" he asked next. I could tell that he was game, as I'd thought he'd be from the start. He was always game, up for a fuck on the balcony or a wild trip to a lonely island. Sasha had said, "So romantic."

Who was I to say no?

But I *did* say no.

To myself. I said *No fucking way* as I looked at my reflection in the mirror. What would I do without a bathroom? Without a mirror? What if I got food in my teeth? How would I floss?

"You're superficial," I told myself, and I agreed wildly with me. Yes, superficial. Yes, I like the soft fluffy towels and the Rembrandt toothpaste and the fabric softener and the scent of

Febreeze. I'd choose walking on a treadmill any day over walking on an honest-to-goodness wilderness path. Why couldn't Sasha have given us a trip to the Four Seasons hotel? Why did she have to want to remake me in her own image? If I were to do the same things to her, I'd flat-iron her frizzy hair, buy her a bikini wax, give her a full-on spa treatment; throw away her butt-ugly shoes.

A jet to a six-seater to a scooter to a boat to a bike became my mantra. Over the next few days, whenever I caught myself relaxing, that image would find a way into my thoughts, and fresh panic would fill me. How could I go through with the trip? Why would I want to spend my anniversary in a humid hell, where my hair would go back to its natural jungle state and there'd be no place to plug in my iron?

Adrien didn't appear to have the same sort of worries at all. He seemed to enjoy the thought of our impending vacation. If anything, he reveled in taunting me.

"Don't forget to pack the netting," he said, and while I thought he meant French Net, he really meant *mosquito* net. What do you bring to a place with no power? There'd be no coffee brewing. No hair-dryer. No stereo. I like my accessories. I like to sit on the floor of the bathroom and dry my hair while reading fashion magazines. I am a city mouse. I've never wanted to be a country mouse. But what had started as a notion for our anniversary—"You'll love it," Sasha said, "You need it"—had turned into something of a challenge.

"Let's go through the list together," Adrien offered, "and I'll spank you for any item you've left out of the bags."

That was more my speed, and I draped myself over his lap as he lifted the paddle, punishing me for the shortsightedness on my part to have forgotten pills to disinfect the water and extra matches so we could light our own fires.

The paddle cut the air, landing with a stinging blow on my tender cheeks as Adrien chuckled at my failures: failure to accept that we were going to a jungle, that running out of hairspray would be the least of our worries.

He spanked me with the same fierce determination with which he approaches every project, and soon I was beyond wet, forgetting why he was slapping my ass with the paddle and wanting only for him to stop so he could fuck me.

But when he pushed me off his lap, he didn't do what I hoped. Instead, he spread out the contents of my suitcase on the floor. And then he couldn't control the laughter. My pretty sundresses, my strappy sandals, my contact lenses: all were shoved into a heap as Adrien repacked for me.

A humid sensation settled over my shoulders, weighing me down when I looked back into my bag: beige, bland, boring. The suitcase could have been packed by Sasha.

"Do you have everything you need?" my sister asked the night before our departure. She and Jarred had invited us to their favorite vegan restaurant.

"I think so," I lied, worried stiff.

"Remember the citronella candles," Sasha said knowingly.

"And mosquito repellent," her husband advised over our after-dinner chais. I noticed they were both still scratching their many different bites. Sasha had a welt on her shoulder the size of a silver dollar. "Spider bite," she said with what I sensed was pride. I wore my own welts under the short pleated skirt. Ones Adrien had given me.

I'd rather be paddled, I thought, *than paddle a boat.*

Would I even survive?

A jet to a plane to a scooter to a boat to a bike.

"This will be good for you," Sasha said, and I wondered why

all the things I dislike seem to have that stamp on them: tofu, wheatgrass juice, flaxseed; things that Sasha lives for. I looked at the welt on her arm and shuddered.

The night we were leaving, Adrien drove us to the airport in our little convertible, parking as close to the runway as we could get. I didn't question why he hadn't driven us to long-term parking, didn't ask him what he was doing when he set his seat all the way back. Somehow, I simply knew he wanted me to climb on top of him.

I pulled up my traveling dress, the one that the catalog had promised would not wrinkle no matter how many times the fabric was torqued and twisted. My plan had been to change to jeans before the trip in the six-seater. I lost my panties in our wheel well and pushed my way on top of Adrien's cock.

He gripped me, pulling me down on him hard, then lifting me back up. As always, his cock took me away with the feeling of being split open by him, of being connected to him in the most primal way. We didn't need to leave the city to find ourselves. We were right here. I thought of our best-laid plans, the plane to the plane to the scooter—and then the roar of a jet overhead made me stop thinking. My hair stood up on the back of my neck. Goose bumps prickled my skin.

This was by far the loudest sound I'd ever heard, a throb that seemed to start within me and radiate out to my toes, to the tips of my straight-ironed hair. As the plane took off overhead, Adrien fucked me faster, lifting me up in the air with the power of his thrusts. I could tell that he was groaning, but I couldn't hear a sound except the roar of the plane. And I realized that I don't ever want total quiet. I don't need darkness. Lights at the end of a runway are among my favorite sights. Landing at SFO thrills me—the sight of the city spread out twinkling on the ground, like glittering multicolored jewels on a party dress.

"Fuck me," Adrien mouthed. I could see his lips move, but I couldn't hear a word. I pounded my body against his and fucked him just as hard as he was taking me, slammed my body to his.

The next jet took off overhead as I found my stride.

He worked me until we were both covered with a sheen of sweat. We came together as another engine shook the ground around us. I saw in his eyes that he never had planned on making me go through with the trip. He'd simply gotten the mileage out of going along with the game.

Maybe next time we'll make the plane—the big plane to the little plane to the scooter to the boat to the bike. But tonight, we just watched the jets take off as Adrien ripped our tickets into tiny pieces and let the confetti flutter off in the breeze.

FLIGHTS OF FANCY

Geneva King

Morning, Cheryl."

"Aubrey!" Cheryl hugged her longtime friend and copilot. "Today is the day! Aren't you excited?" She kissed a trail down Aubrey's cheeks.

Aubrey laughed and wiggled free from Cheryl's embrace. "I've been looking forward to this all year."

The two pilots settled into their seats. Cheryl prepared the plane while Aubrey flipped through the passenger list.

"Marjorie and Cynthia...Tom and Eliza...Jane came back. I'll be glad to see her again."

"Did Toni make it? I know she was wavering for a while."

Aubrey scanned the list. "I don't see her name. Didn't she just have a baby?" Her eyebrows furrowed.

Cheryl caught the look and reached over to stroke her cheek. "What? Your ex signed up?"

Aubrey shook her head. "God, don't joke about that. Do you know Eric and Linda Brown?"

* * *

When the attendant announced boarding, Linda grabbed her husband's hand and pulled him into the line.

To his credit, he didn't protest the rough treatment. It had been his lack of attention that had made the last thirteen hours of her life pure misery. Give men a simple task and they manage to screw it up every time.

Luckily, with a little finagling, she'd managed to secure tickets on the next flight to Florida at no extra cost. The clerk had seemed quite reluctant, something about a luxury trip, but once Linda had assured the girl and her manager that she'd go through as many channels as possible to make their lives a living hell, they'd wisely given in.

It was one more reason she didn't fly on small airlines. They weren't professional enough. Even now, the line was moving entirely too slowly. The woman taking tickets seemed to know everyone in line and found it necessary to hug and chat with each passenger going through.

Linda felt Eric start to fidget. She kicked his ankle. "Just remember, this was your idea."

He sighed. "I heard it was a good airline."

Linda snorted. "From who? Roger?"

He wrenched his arm away. "Julie, actually. Look, just chill out. We'll get there soon enough!"

Linda sucked in a deep breath. She honestly had no idea how her parents had survived thirty-nine years of marriage. She'd endured one and was already looking forward to widowhood.

When they finally reached the ticket stand, Linda mustered up her most disapproving look and held out her ticket.

The stewardess peered at the couple, then looked at their tickets. "Are you in the right place?"

Linda bristled. "Of course we are."

Eric smiled at her. "We got bumped from an earlier flight."

The stewardess looked worried, but tore off the ticket and handed back the stubs. "Enjoy your trip."

Linda tossed her hair and marched past the gate. She pulled Eric close. " 'Are you sure you're in the right place?' Honestly, what's up with these people?"

Eric opened his mouth to reply, but Linda was too deep into her tirade to notice.

"I don't know where they get their help from. Next year, I'll take care of the arrangements like I should have done to begin with."

Eric grabbed her arm and pulled her off to the side. "Would you stop bitching for one second?"

Linda stared at his hand.

He released her. "It's our first anniversary. We're supposed to be having a good time."

"You're right. We are. In Florida. Are we in Florida? No, we're stuck in airport hell!" Linda pushed past him to board the plane.

A flight attendant greeted them. "Hi, I'm Krista. Welcome aboard."

If forced, Linda would admit that the airline wasn't lying about luxury. The large seats were grouped in twos or threes. Each passenger had plenty of legroom.

Eric nudged her. "Not bad, huh?"

Linda pretended she didn't hear him as she settled in. She wasn't ready to let him off the hook, no matter how comfortable the accommodations were. And they were; Linda sank into her chair with a tiny sigh. She hadn't realized how tight her back had become after spending the night on those rigid airport benches.

Her enjoyment was short-lived. The other passengers came down the aisle, loudly shouting greetings to those around them.

Linda popped an eye open to watch the activity around her. Two ladies found seats next to them. The brunette in a short skirt chatted with the passengers behind her, while her partner, a blonde butch, loaded their bags overhead.

The camaraderie was getting to Linda. "Why do they all know each other?"

Eric shrugged. "Maybe they're a tour group."

The pilot's voice came over the intercom. "Welcome everyone to our 2008 retreat! Aubrey and I are so glad to see so many of you back with us. Expected flight time is six hours and twenty-two minutes. We'll be taking off in a few moments, so just sit back and relax. And people, be patient until the seat belt sign goes off. There will be plenty of time for fun once we get in the air."

The other passengers laughed. The couple across the aisle winked at each other.

Linda turned to her husband. "I guess that explains how they know each other."

"Before we start our safety briefing, I have an announcement. Two of our passengers, Eric and Linda Brown, are celebrating their first anniversary with us today! Let's give them a round of applause."

The other passengers clapped and Eric waved his thanks.

"How the hell did they know about that?" Linda whispered.

Eric looked pleased. "I told them when you went to the bathroom." He kissed her forehead. "Happy anniversary."

"I knew I shouldn't have let you out of my sight." Linda frowned, but snuggled closer to her husband and kissed his cheek. "Men."

She'd hoped to get some sleep once they were in the air, but the other passengers showed no signs of quieting down. She tossed in the seat and sighed loudly, hoping someone would get the hint.

Instead a twangy voice hit her ears. "Y'all must be new. I don't remember seeing you here before. I'm Marjorie. Happy anniversary, by the way."

Eric thanked her. "First time on this airline."

Linda tried to kick him. They wouldn't be quiet if he encouraged the conversation.

Eric didn't seem to get the hint. "So, what's this retreat about? We were wondering why everyone seemed to know each other." The woman didn't immediately answer and Linda caught herself waiting for the reply.

"So, you didn't sign up for the trip?"

"No, we got booted off an earlier flight and the airline put us on this one instead."

"Oh." Marjorie chuckled. "Well, you all will get a real interesting way to celebrate."

Linda's curiosity got the best of her. She opened her eyes and sat up. "Why do you say that?"

The woman started. "Goodness, I thought you were sleeping."

"I was trying." Linda tried not to sound as bitchy as she felt.

"My fault. Everyone's so excited. But I'll let you get your rest." She winked. "I bet you lovebirds probably need it."

Linda turned to Eric. "You know, that didn't answer my question."

He wrapped his arm around her. "Go to sleep, I know you need it."

Linda woke to Eric's elbow jabbing her repeatedly in the side. "What—"

He clamped a hand over her mouth. "Be quiet. I want to show you something."

She glared, but nodded assent. He pointed to the two women in the row next to them.

It took her a moment to realize what she was seeing. The girl closest to her lay back against the chair with a blanket across her lap. Linda thought she was sleeping until she noticed her fingers were clenching the armrest. Her partner sat next to her, head snuggled above her chest. One arm disappeared under the blanket. Linda realized it led right between the brunette's legs.

Linda removed Eric's hand and leaned across him to get a closer look. Now that she knew what was happening, she could pick up on the steady movements of the hand under the blanket, the subtle twitches of the girl being pleasured. Her shirt had been unbuttoned and as she arched her back, Linda got an eyeful of her cleavage.

"What the hell?" she whispered.

The butch heard her. She looked up and winked at Linda before kissing the top of her girlfriend's exposed breast. Without breaking eye contact, she tugged the dark shirt to the side and captured a nipple beneath her teeth. The girl groaned and bucked frantically. Her head rolled to the side, but Linda doubted she was aware of anything but the orgasm building up inside of her.

"Lin, got another one."

With a last look at the brunette, she turned her head and peered between the seats. A mop of short blonde hair bobbed up and down in a man's lap. Her tongue twirled around his fat cock, leaving a shiny trail of saliva down the shaft. The man grunted; his fingers entwined in her hair. As Linda watched, he guided her head down his penis, until her lips made contact with its hairy base.

A deep cry pulled Linda's attention to the other side of the plane. Two men sat next to each other. A dark-skinned girl sat astride one, hips bucking frantically as she rode him. The other licked her bare nipples and played with her asshole. She looked at her husband, but his gaze was fixed on the threesome.

His hand caressed the growing bulge in his jeans.

"Eric."

"Hmm?" He didn't look at her, but rubbed his erection harder as the girl humped her partner more vigorously.

"Eric!" She grabbed him until he turned to face her. "What the hell are we going to do?"

He reached for her. "When in Rome..."

She swatted his hand away. "Stop it. Where's our stewardess? She's got to know about this."

Eric peered into the aisle. "I could be wrong, but I think that's her four aisles up. And I think she knows."

Linda slumped back in the chair. Every seat on the plane sported people either having sex or watching another couple. Moans came from the row in front; Linda assumed Marjorie must be having her own fun but she didn't want to look.

She turned back to the lesbians beside them. The brunette had come. The butch stroked her face, while kissing and whispering to her. Suddenly, Linda felt incredibly left out. Here she was on her anniversary, her first in fact, and not only had she not had sex of any kind, she'd spent most of it fighting with her husband. And over what? A misdirected flight?

The butch caught her eye and said something to her girlfriend. The brunette glanced at them over her shoulder and smiled.

Linda averted her eyes, embarrassed to be caught staring at such a personal moment.

"It's okay."

Linda turned back. "What?"

"I said it's okay." The butch smiled and nipped her girlfriend's ear. "She likes to be watched."

The brunette giggled. "She does, too." She extended her hand across the aisle. Her blouse was still open and a breast spilled out. "I'm Terri. This is Sue."

Eric shook her hand, his eyes never leaving her exposed chest. "Eric and Linda."

Terri smiled. "Linda's a pretty name. It suits you."

"Thanks," Linda replied, chagrined to find her voice sounded shy. "I mean, it works."

"Yeah. So what are you guys into?"

"Excuse me?"

"I mean, do you like to be watched, or are you more the voyeuristic type?"

Linda's cheeks were getting warmer. She couldn't seem to pull her gaze from Terri's nipple. "Umm, nothing. I mean, normal stuff."

Sue bit her lover's shoulder. "I think I know what she needs."

"What?" Linda snapped.

"How'd you like her to eat your pussy?"

"No!" Linda blurted the response without thinking. "I mean, don't you think you should ask her that?"

"She loves to do it. Tell her, baby?"

Terri nodded, her eyes brightening. "It'd be my pleasure."

Linda shook her head. This was getting too weird for her. "I'll pass. But…thanks."

Terri looked disappointed and when Linda looked at Eric, he did too.

"You should give it a try," he whispered.

"She's a girl," she hissed back, trying to keep her voice low.

"So? Aren't you the one who said girls could do it better?"

She looked at him incredulously. "That was college! I don't know them. And we're on an airplane!"

"Along with the rest of Orgy Central." He kissed her forehead. "I bet you'd look totally hot with her between your legs. Think of it as my anniversary present."

Linda looked back at Terri's eager face and the rest of her

arguments disappeared. She was horny. Why should she be the only one not getting any?

"Fine. Okay, I guess so. Why not?"

Terri scrambled out of her chair. Eric kissed his wife and relinquished his seat. He settled in next to Sue.

Linda tried to smile at the brunette standing over her. "Hi," she squeaked.

Terri slowly rubbed Linda's thighs. "Relax, Linda."

"You know," she heard Eric say to Sue, "I think this is the first time the whole trip she's been silent."

With a swift yank, Terri pulled Linda to the edge of the plush seat. She knelt in the aisle and started unbuckling Linda's pants.

Linda became aware of the passengers around them turning to see what was happening. *So,* she thought, *the watcher becomes the watched.* She threw her arms over her face to block the others out.

Linda's legs were pushed apart and Terri's warm breath flowed over her pussy. Her hips lifted up, anxious to feel the woman's mouth. Terri obliged with a light flick of the tongue across her hole. She moaned and her legs fell farther apart.

"That's it, sweetheart. Let her pleasure you."

Linda moved her arms to see a strange hand caressing her. Marjorie had turned around and was watching with unabashed curiosity. Linda glanced down at Terri; all she could see was the top of the woman's streaked hair. It was odd looking down and knowing that the person sending shocks through her body was female.

Terri made good on her promise. In a few short minutes, Linda lay clutching Marjorie's hand, while she begged for release.

"Oh my god." Terri's tongue pressed against her clit and she came with a loud moan.

"Was I right?" Sue stood behind Terri and massaged her shoulders.

Linda nodded, too weak to do much else. "She's great."

Terri climbed on Linda and kissed her on the mouth. After a moment's hesitation, Linda kissed her back. Linda allowed herself to explore the other woman's body, the soft curves of her back and shoulders, her round cheeks. Everything was so different from Eric's muscles.

Sue bent over Terri. Her pants were gone; instead a purple dildo jutted from her pelvis. She wound one hand in Terri's hair and pulled her back toward her. Linda watched the passion between the two, the delight in their touch, and suddenly missed her husband. Eric wasn't a bad guy when it came down to it, just a tad bit irresponsible at times. But he always tried to be good to her and put up with her crap, which she had been dishing out more than normal lately.

She looked past the couple for her husband. Eric was sitting in the same seat, but now their stewardess sat on his lap, skirt hiked around her waist. Her hips swiveled, driven by the rhythm of his fingers plunging into her.

All her loving thoughts flew out of her mind as she watched the girl bounce and squeal. If she wasn't mistaken, he had wanted to watch. He never said anything about entertaining some shrieking floozy.

He caught her watching him. "I love you," he mouthed.

She glowered, but blew him a kiss and turned back to Terri. Sue pressed her back onto Linda's body and pushed the dildo into her.

Linda gripped Terri's body and clutched her tightly as Sue thrust. Every pump went through Linda, and as Terri came, Linda felt the spasms reverberate through her body.

Sue lifted Terri off Linda and cradled her limp body in the

aisle. The stewardess had moved on to another man, leaving Eric alone. His hand rubbed his erection; he hadn't come either. Linda decided to make her move before someone else did.

"Hey, Eric." She shook her foot at him. "Need some help?"

He jumped up and dropped his pants. Linda got a quick glimpse of his throbbing cock before he climbed on top of her.

He paused—the head of his penis pressed against her hole. "You sure?"

"Come on." She groaned as he slid inside her. "After all, when in Rome..."

Cheryl pulled into the gate and hit the intercom button. "Ladies and gentlemen, welcome to Miami. For those of you continuing on with us, the bus will be waiting outside of the baggage claim. Everyone else, enjoy your time in Florida."

Aubrey hopped in Cheryl's lap and grabbed the mike. "Take your time getting to the bus; we might be a bit late." They heard a loud cheer from the cabin.

"She's so naughty, isn't she?" Cheryl giggled and disconnected. "I didn't think I was going to make it all six hours."

Aubrey kissed her. "A few more minutes and we're free to fuck as we please." They opened the door to watch the passengers deplane. The new couple walked down the aisle, holding hands.

Krista winked at the man and wished them a safe trip. "Goodbye Eric, Linda. I hope you fly with us again."

Eric looked at Linda, who smiled slowly. "Count on it."

THE GIRL MOST LIKELY

Kristina Wright

Cindy Harris?"

I jolted at hearing my name—my maiden name—spoken by a deep male voice as I settled into my seat. The plane was crowded, I was trying to avoid hitting anyone in the head with my overstuffed carry-on, and the last thing I needed was to spend an eight-hour flight to London chatting it up with an old high school chum.

Then I looked at him and was taken back fifteen years, to my senior year in high school and my first true love.

His face had changed, though I supposed mine had, as well. I knew my hair was different—longer and darker than the short blonde cut I'd had back then—but he had recognized me immediately while I wasn't sure I would have picked him out of a crowd.

"Don't tell me you've forgotten me," he said with that old familiar smirk.

I found myself smiling in response. "Max Viannetti. Wow."

"Yeah, wow."

We were interrupted by the flight attendant coming by to make sure our tray tables were up and our seats were in the upright position. After she passed by, I shook my head. "This is surreal. I haven't seen you since—"

"Prom."

I winced. Yeah, I'd kind of forgotten that our sweet love affair had ended on a sour note.

"Water under the bridge," he said, his voice unlike what I remembered, but the tilt of his head as familiar as my own reflection. "How are you?"

I hesitated, then closed my eyes wearily. "Loaded question. I'm supposed to say 'fine,' right?"

He laughed. "It's a long flight. I think you can say more than 'fine.'"

I felt the prick of embarrassing and inappropriate tears behind my eyelids. I knew my eyes were glistening brightly when I looked at him and his concerned expression told me I wasn't doing a good job of faking joy.

"Hey, sorry. I didn't mean to—"

I waved him off. "No, I'm just tired. It's been a long month. I just got divorced."

The word was bitter and hot on my tongue, though I'd had more than a year to get used to it. Blurting it out to a man I hadn't seen in fifteen years and had parted ways with under less than the best of circumstances just reinforced how utterly worn out I was these days.

"Sorry to hear that," he said, and sounded sincere. "Been there, done that, myself. It's miserable, even when it's necessary."

I nodded. That summed it up. "Anyway, I'm off to London for a much-needed holiday. How about you?"

"Wedding," he said with a grimace. "My best friend from law school."

"I didn't know you were an attorney." I felt an overwhelming sense of sadness. Max had once been an integral part of my everyday life. I had loved him, once; probably still did in that way that young love never really dies.

"I'm not," he said. "I teach law. Decided early on I preferred theory to practice."

"Smart man."

Somehow, I had missed the fact that we had taxied and taken off. Me, who hated flying and got nauseous on takeoff and landing, had missed the worst part. I smiled at Max.

"I'm glad I ran into you. It's nice to catch up."

And catch up, we did. For the next two hours, through our rather unappetizing dinner, we talked—about law school for him and design school for me, his failed marriage and mine, mutual friends from high school who had drifted in and out of each of our lives—we talked about everything but the past.

As I nestled into my seat with a blanket over my lap and an airline pillow jammed against the headrest, trying to get comfortable enough to sleep postdinner, Max raised the armrest between us. I jumped at the touch of his hand on my thigh, a sense of the unfamiliar colliding with some very intense memories. His soft chuckle made me relax.

"I was a jerk back then," he said softly, the first reference to our history he'd made since we'd started talking. "An arrogant jackass who thought I was entitled to score on prom night, if no other time."

I felt my face flush hotly. It wasn't something I wanted to rehash. I'd been a good girl in high school—a good girl who didn't believe in premarital sex. That had only lasted until the second semester of freshman year at Georgetown when I succumbed to what I believed was love and had a lackluster experience. I had spent a long time regretting saying no to Max so many nights and losing him because of it. It really wasn't something I wanted to talk about.

I turned my head toward the aisle. "S'okay," I mumbled. "I was a goody-goody who thought I was saving myself for something better."

"We had some fun though," he said, his voice stirring something inside me. "Didn't we?"

Memories of fevered nights of long make-out sessions and roaming hands—his *and* mine—flitted through my brain. I nodded. "Yeah, we did." He fell silent then and, like the rest of the plane, we slept.

I awoke from an erotic dream, disoriented for a moment until the loud, steady hum of the plane became real again. What was also real was the big, warm hand resting on my thigh. I glanced at Max, sound asleep and sprawled in his seat—as sprawled as anyone can get in an airplane seat—his face in sleep slack and peaceful, hints of the youth I once knew in the lock of hair slipping boyishly down his forehead.

I don't know what made me reach out and touch his mouth, but one moment I was watching him sleep and the next I was brushing my index finger over his full lips—lips that had driven me out of my mind when I was too inexperienced to know what I had been missing. Still caught in the web of my sex dream, I contemplated what that mouth could do to me now. I shivered at the thought.

Memory and fantasy were so intertwined in my tired brain that I didn't realize Max was awake and watching me until his lips parted. The quick lick of his tongue against the tip of my finger made me jerk back in surprise.

"I—I'm—I was dreaming," I stammered.

"About me, I hope." His drowsy expression held a hint of lust. Just a hint—as if he had been dreaming, too—but it was enough to make me press my thighs together. "Want to tell me about it?"

I shook my head. "I don't really remember what it was about. Just...that it was about sex and need—I needed something..."

"So it was about me."

I didn't take offense at his comment. The scenario probably had been related to Max, but even my dreaming self couldn't conjure up what it would be like to sleep with Max because it had never happened.

"Yeah, probably."

He shifted so that his mouth was very close to my ear. "You know what's funny? I bitched about not being able to fuck you but you're the only woman I ever dream about like that."

I looked at him, trying to sniff out the mockery. He looked utterly sincere. "Really?"

His hand stroked my thigh and I jerked against him as if he were stroking my bare pussy. The past was so close to the surface, I knew exactly what his fingers would feel like on my skin. But there was a blanket and skirt between me and those fingers.

"Yeah," he said, staring at me so intently I felt like he could see my thoughts. "Really."

The plane was quiet except for the hum of the engine; everyone around us was asleep and only a couple of overhead lights illuminated night owls several rows away. The flight attendants were nowhere to be seen, no doubt catching up on the gossip before having to serve the next round of beverages. I felt something like anticipation thrumming in my veins—anticipation and a long-dormant desire. I hadn't known what to do with it when I was in high school, but I knew now.

I took Max's hand off the blanket that covered my lap. The flicker of disappointment on his face immediately turned to one of interest when I lifted the blanket and returned his hand to my thigh. I felt him reach down to toy with the hem of my skirt, at last touching bare skin. I sighed and closed my eyes.

"Remember all those nights on your parents' couch?" he whispered. "That dance we did every time? Touching, pulling back—all that teasing."

"I wasn't teasing," I said. "I was trying to be good."

He slid my skirt up an inch. If this had been high school, I would have let him go just to midthigh, then I would have pushed him away and sent him home. Now it was all I could do not to beg him to fuck me right there on the plane.

"You *were* good. The girl most likely to be good." He shook his head. "And I was the poor, love-struck fool who thought I could corrupt you."

"I'm not that girl anymore." I reached under the blanket and jerked my skirt up until his entire hand rested on my bare skin. "And I'm not sure what I'm most likely to do, but I know what I want to do."

He curved his hand around my thigh, high enough that I could feel the barest touch against the edge of my panties. I squirmed, tilting my hips as much as the seat belt would allow—which wasn't much—and looked at him.

"What are you doing?" he said, but it was not an admonishment. "We'll get arrested and be banned from the airline for life."

I sighed. "Oh, c'mon, Mr. Law Professor, don't be a prude."

"Believe me, I'm not feeling very prudish," he said, his voice barely a whisper. "I just can't do to you what I want to do."

"That never stopped you from trying."

That was all it took. Max shifted toward me and slid his

hand over my panty-covered crotch. The heat was so intense I whimpered. Though the noise of the plane drowned out the sound, he looked at me sternly.

"Hush, or I'll stop."

I licked my bottom lip and was rewarded with a barely perceptible groan. "Don't stop until I come."

Roughly, he slid his hand under the waistband of my panties and touched me. He was using his left hand and the position was awkward, with his elbow lodged uncomfortably beneath my breasts, but it didn't seem to matter when his middle finger found my clit. I clutched at his wrist, needing to touch him and not just be touched. I moved my hand down until it covered his, resting against my pussy, pressing against my clit. I rubbed his hand and he rubbed me.

"Like that?" He stroked me and I tried not to moan. "You like that?"

I bit my lip to keep from making a sound and nodded. I wanted to fling myself on top of him, run my hands all over his body, sink down onto his cock, but I was limited to this—his hand on my mound, his middle finger pressed against my clit in the confines of the airplane.

I reached between us and unfastened my seat belt. Without the restraint, I was able to slide a little lower, spread my thighs a little wider....

Max made a *tsking* sound in my ear. "You're supposed to keep your seat belt fastened at all times."

I grinned wickedly as I pressed his hand between my thighs. "I told you I wasn't a good girl anymore."

My smile faded to a look of surprise as he slid his middle finger inside me. I felt my pussy clench involuntarily and couldn't contain a gasp of desire. I clutched at his hand, guiding him with urgency as he rubbed my pussy with short, but hard, strokes.

The palm of his hand rested against my clit—not enough pressure to get me off, but enough to keep me in a state of near orgasmic arousal.

"You're so fucking wet. I knew you would be if I ever touched you like this," he whispered.

We were shoulder to shoulder because of the angle and the narrow seats, his body kept a little away from me because he would have to move his hand if he shifted closer and I needed that hand where it was. I needed to come.

We both froze as a flight attendant passed by, Max's finger pressed inside me, my spread thighs barely concealed by the flimsy blanket. But she didn't even glance our way and, after a moment, she passed back to her station and Max resumed playing with me.

"Tell me what you need," he whispered. "I want to get you off."

I trembled at his words. We might not have been in the most intimate of positions or locations, but his words were doing as much to get me off as his finger. I shifted, frustrated at the confines of my seat and the bad angle.

"More, another finger," I told him. "And keep talking to me."

Immediately, I felt him slide his index finger inside me along with his middle finger. I brushed my own fingertips against the back of his hand and down over his knuckles, wet with my desire. If there had been room, I would have added my finger to his two—to feel both of us inside me, surrounded by my wetness.

"Better? Feel full?"

I nodded.

"Wish it was my cock inside you instead of my fingers?"

I jerked up against his hand. "Yes," I said with a whispered hiss. "Oh god, yes."

"Good. Think about my cock fucking you," he said as

he stroked me harder. "Think about it as you come on my fingers."

That was all it took. I clenched my thighs around his hand, a mental picture of his cock—which I had never even seen—driving into me. I bit down on my lip until I tasted blood, eyes closed so I could pretend we were alone as I rocked as little as possible against the fingers inside me.

"I feel you," he whispered. "You're grabbing on to me. Your pussy is so wet, but you're still clinging to me."

Max kept talking to me, whispering sexy, naughty things as my orgasm went on and on. It was as if my body, limited by our surroundings and position, was taking as long to finish coming as it had taken to get to orgasm. Softly panting, I relaxed my grip on Max's wrist, realizing that I had been digging my nails into him the entire time.

"Sorry," I said, rubbing the indentations my nails had left behind. "I was kind of lost there for a minute."

He slowly withdrew his fingers, rubbing them over my pussy. "Don't worry about it. That was amazing."

I shook my head. "You have no idea."

There was a moment of awkward silence punctuated by yet another flight attendant pass-by. This time, she looked pointedly at us. Her expression was neutral, but the wink gave her away.

I sunk lower in my seat, mortified. "Oh hell, she knows."

"There's still some of that good girl left in you," Max said.

I shifted in my seat, tugging my skirt down over my hips. I smiled wickedly at him as I slipped my hand into his lap and stroked his erection through his pants. The motion was so familiar I knew exactly how he would react. This time, though, I knew I wasn't going to be content with a little groping and fantasizing.

"I bet you could have me thoroughly corrupted by the time

we leave London," I said, giving his cock a little squeeze.

By the time we made our descent into Heathrow, the butterflies in my stomach had nothing at all to do with flying.

BERT AND BETTY

Ryan Field

At nine o'clock in the morning, the Philadelphia International Airport was fairly busy. The wide brown corridors were packed with people, there were long lines at the newsstands, and the food court was all lit up and ready to serve. All of the gates were admitting flights. Their signboards were filled and their rows of gray chairs occupied and noisy.

But Betty Culp was far enough away from all this confusion, at the back end of the airport, to take a deep breath and inhale the freshly showered, spicy aroma of the guy standing in front of her. They were boarding a flight to Kearny, Nebraska, and there weren't many people going *there* that day. She could see that most of the people on the flight were business travelers, and that they were all carrying briefcases, light and simple, to their destinations. And the guy in front of her, a young man in his early thirties, with short, dark hair and wide, solid shoulders, was rocking on the balls of his feet as he inched toward the gate with a black raincoat over his arm. He kept fidgeting with a thick, gold wedding band on his right hand as if it either hurt, or itched, his ring finger.

When Betty discovered a few minutes later that the same awkward guy was seated right next to her, she lowered her head and sighed as she slipped past his stocky legs to claim her seat. He had the aisle, and she had the window. Why couldn't he have been bald and fat? Why couldn't they just seat her next to someone's grandmother for once? The plane was almost empty; she could have had two seats to herself. Just when she swore that she was going to be good in the air, and that she wasn't going to seduce one more guy on a commercial flight again, fate had placed her in another tempting situation.

He wore a dark business suit, with a pale blue shirt and a yellow tie, but you could see his body was muscular and stocky: like a professional baseball player. He sat with his legs spread wide and his big feet crossed at the ankles; he was one of those steak and potatoes types, who looked a bit out of place in anything other than worn jeans and a T-shirt. Betty sat next to him and crossed her legs like a proper lady. She was wearing a short beige skirt that day, with fawn leather pumps and no stockings. It was August and her long, thin legs were tanned and smooth. She hardly ever bothered with underwear.

They buckled their seat belts, and she noticed that his bulky hands gripped the arms of the seat with thick, long fingers. His skin was tanned, too, so his knuckles didn't turn white, but he clenched tightly until the plane was finally in midair. She couldn't help laughing when he took a deep breath after the captain announced that everyone could unbuckle their belts. "I guess you don't fly often," she said. "That was a pretty smooth takeoff."

He smiled and rubbed his strong chin. "Ah well, actually, I hate to fly. And I never do it unless it's absolutely necessary. But I guess I'm going to have to get used to flying about once a month now. My ex-wife just moved back to Nebraska to be with her family, with my two kids, and I don't have much of a choice." His voice was deep and hoarse and he kept shaking his right knee up and down.

She smiled. "Trust me, you'll get used to it. I fly all the time." When she smoothed her skirt she noticed that he stared at her legs for a moment. At least he was divorced, but she still wasn't sure if he was remarried because of the wedding band.

"Are the flights to Nebraska always this empty?" he asked. He looked around the plane and motioned with his left arm. The seats behind them and in front of them were empty, and there were two college-age boys sitting across from them in the middle row listening to their iPods. "This is almost like a private charter flight, when you think about it."

"You really never know," Betty said. "Sometimes the flights are jammed, other times they *are* empty. That's the one rule I've learned about flying: you never can predict anything." And she was an expert, too. As the marketing director for a large chemical company, Betty had flown the world by the time she was thirty years old. She'd also blown half the world, too. She discovered early in her career that men who travel a lot by plane are usually walking around the airports with semi-erections in their Brooks Brothers slacks.

"I'm Bert," he said, and then extended his right hand.

She reached for it, and smiled. "I'm Betty. Nice to meet you." When she softly squeezed his hand, their eyes met; he stared for a moment and then jerked his head and smiled. And that's when she secretly predicted she would be able to get into his pants before the flight was over.

Bert began to tell her the story of his bad marriage, while she folded her arms across her chest and pretended to be interested. When he told her about how his ex-wife suddenly announced one afternoon that she was bored and needed to explore her "inner self," Betty sighed, but she was staring at the rough stubble on his jaw and wondering what it would be like to rub her soft boobs against it. And when he told her that his ex-wife decided to take a cooking class so she could learn how to make *pumpkin ravioli* and broaden her horizons, Betty just shook her head and frowned. She was really concentrating on Bert's large fingers and wondering if his penis was just as large. He said his ex-wife was a fan of the television show "The Office," and that she actually decided to leave him on the night he went to bed early and refused to watch the season finale with her. He pressed his hands on his knees, and asked, "How do you like that? She left because I didn't stay up to watch the season finale of 'The Office'...and I was freaking tired that night!"

"Ah well, there you are," Betty said. "I guess some women want the world." She pushed a strand of long blonde hair away from her face and smiled. But she was really wondering what kind of dumb bitch would force her poor husband to watch a TV show like "The Office." She'd watched it once or twice; she hated it.

Bert lifted his right hand and waved it. "And now I can't even get this damn ring off my finger. I'll have to have it cut off eventually. We were married for ten years and I gained about twenty pounds since the wedding."

"Well, there you are. What with all that pumpkin ravioli that's understandable," Betty said. "But I think you look fine; very athletic and strong." She reached over and gently squeezed his bicep.

But he missed the compliment. "Oh, please. She couldn't cook to save her own life. She only *took* cooking courses...there's a difference." He stretched his wide legs forward and leaned his head on the back of the seat. "I'm going to try to get some sleep;

besides, I've been boring you long enough. No one likes to hear ex-wife stories, and I don't normally tell them."

"Don't be silly," Betty said, "I'm happy to have the conversation." She was always amazed at how some men never got the subtlest of hints. There she was, practically licking her lips to get a taste of what he had between his legs, and all he cared about was a nap. So she reached down to *her* lap for her purse and purposely spilled the contents between Bert's legs. "I'm so sorry," she said. "I'm such a mess."

Bert smiled, but when he looked down between his legs his eyes bugged out and his jaw dropped. Beside her lip gloss and bronzer, just next to her small makeup mirror, he saw a small red dildo. You couldn't miss it: a rubbery latex penis, about five inches long, leaning against his testicles.

Betty pressed her hand to her throat. "Sorry...it's my secret travel companion, is all." Then she reached between his legs and started to fish for the contents of her purse. She gathered her makeup, and purposely rubbed the side of her hand against the inside of Bert's thigh. When she reached for the red dildo, he jerked because she took a handful of his balls instead. "Are you okay?" she asked.

"Ah well..." he said. His eyes were closed by then, and he started to wiggle his legs.

She began to massage his testicles; they were large and filled her hand. "Why don't you just sit back and relax for a while? I'm not usually this forward with strange men, but you are so attractive," she said. But it was a bold lie. She'd done this before, with many guys, either in an airport or on a plane.

Bert's eyes were rolling and his mouth was half open. "Is this okay? I mean, we could get in trouble for this." But he didn't look up to see if anyone was watching them while she stroked his balls in public.

"The plane is empty," she whispered. "No one is watching. Just close your eyes, handsome."

The higher her hand went, the harder his penis became. She looked up for a moment to see if anyone could see her groping between his legs. The flight attendants were sitting way up front, and everyone else seemed to be minding his or her own business. But when she licked her bottom lip and began to unzip his slacks, she looked across to the next row of seats and saw that one of the young men who had been listening to music earlier was now watching every move she made. He had reddish blond hair, fair white skin, and a cute little pug nose. He couldn't have been more than twenty-one. They stared at each other for a moment, and then he smiled, spread his long legs and rubbed his own crotch. Betty winked at him, and then she told Bert to close his eyes and relax. This was an interesting state of affairs; she'd never had an audience while she sucked a guy off on a plane.

When Bert's zipper was down, Betty slowly reached inside his boxer shorts and grabbed his dick. It was completely erect by then, and it pulsed and jumped when she wrapped her palm around the shaft. She pulled it out of his pants carefully, but Bert opened his eyes and looked toward the front of the plane. "I don't know about this," he said. "We could get into trouble." Then he looked across the row to see what the two young guys were doing. Both had their eyes closed and were still listening to their iPods.

"Just close your eyes," she said. "It won't take long. You know you want it."

She leaned toward him and gently jerked his cock a few times; she placed the tip of her thumb against the base of his dickhead and rubbed the soft skin. There was precome already beginning to ooze from the opening. Oh, she knew it wouldn't take too long with this one. The poor guy probably hadn't had good head in years. And if he was so worried about having sex in public, he clearly could have stopped her from continuing.

Bert closed his eyes again and leaned back; he bucked his hips forward so that his dick was standing up, out of his pants. It was thick, and if you wrapped your hand around the base there would still have been four inches showing through the top. "You promise you'll keep looking to see that we don't get caught," he said, but his eyes were still closed.

"Yes, I promise," she said. But when she looked across the row, the young college guy was staring at them again. This time, his blue eyes were glazed and he was jerking his own dick. She smiled at him, opened her mouth, and then went down on Bert's cock while the stranger watched.

She took the dick to the back of her throat; her lips went all the way down to the fabric of his white boxer shorts. His crotch smelled like fresh soap, but there was still a hint of that watered down oil and vinegar stench of a man's sweaty balls. She inhaled deeply through her nose; this was her favorite men's cologne. The young guy across the row licked his palm and wrapped it around his own large erection and slowly began to masturbate. She pressed her tongue against the bottom side of Bert's dick and began to suck. Her cheekbones indented and her lips grew puffy. When she looked up, with a mouthful of cock, to see what the young guy was doing, her eyes opened wider, and then she blinked. The redheaded one who had been masturbating was still watching her suck Bert's dick, but the other guy who had been sleeping was now sucking the redhead off. The other guy had dark brown hair, and his eyes were light brown. When Betty's eyes met the eyes of the other cocksucker, he lifted his hand and slowly waved his fingers. She pressed her tongue hard against Bert's shaft and smiled back.

She went all the way down to the base of Bert's dick again

and began to suck and slurp, pressing her lips together when she reached the head so it would feel more like a hand job than a blow job. Her head bobbed and saliva dripped down her chin. Every so often, when she swallowed, she tasted Bert's salty precome. The dark-haired guy who was sucking off his friend in the opposite row mimicked everything she did. When Betty's head bobbed up and down quickly, so did his; when Betty's cheeks indented, so did his; and when Betty let it pop out of her mouth so she could lick the head, so did he. The red-haired guy who was getting sucked off, and watching Betty suck Bert off, rested his head back on the seat. He stared at Bert's wide dick; his tongue hung out, he bucked his hips and pressed his palm on the back of the dark-haired guy's head.

When the pilot suddenly announced they were heading toward some rough turbulence and that everyone should buckle their seat belts, Betty slid Bert's cock halfway out of her mouth and wrapped her right hand around the base. Bert moaned, "Oh yeah, that's it," while she sucked the head of his dick and jerked him off at the same time. She looked across the row; the other cocksucker was now sucking the head and jerking the shaft of his buddy, too. The dark-haired guy nodded yes, to let her know that his red-haired buddy was about to blow a load, and she began to work harder on Bert's dick, as if she were in a cock-sucking contest and someone would receive a prize.

With her lips wrapped around the top of Bert's dick, her hand worked faster. A moment later Bert was ready to release, and he spread his legs even wider so that one knee was almost out in the aisle. He gripped the arms of his seat and his body went rigid. When he squinted and furrowed his eyebrows, Betty knew his toes were curling inside his black shoes. But more than that, just as Bert was about to orgasm, she looked across the row and the dark-haired guy nodded again. Her broad eyes met his, and then both Bert and the red-haired guy came at the exact same time. Bert shot a load of cream all the way to the back of her throat; she gulped and swallowed. The dark-haired young guy was sucking and swallowing the last ounce from his buddy's dick, too. Betty and the dark-haired guy continued to stare at each other, as if they were watching their own reflections, and went all the way down on their partners' dicks at the same time to make sure they didn't waste a drop of come.

The plane jerked back and forth for a moment, but not much. Betty lifted her head and touched the corners of her mouth with her fingertips to be sure nothing was dripping. While she reached down into her purse for a small mirror, Bert shoved his cock back into his pants and adjusted his legs.

"Ah well," he said. Then he looked around the plane to see if anyone was watching them. The flight attendants were nowhere to be seen, the red-haired guy in the next row was still sleeping, and the dark-haired guy was wiping his chin with a white tissue. Bert smiled at him and waved; the thought of actually receiving a blow job in public, by a great-looking woman, made his heart beat faster.

When Betty looked into the mirror, her lips were puffy. She applied more lip gloss and said, "I guess it's only light turbulence." What else could she say? *Thanks for letting me suck your dick; it was my pleasure. And the two gay guys in the row across from us really enjoyed watching me suck your dick, too.* She knew it was best to get right back to normal, as if none of this had ever happened, which was fine with her.

But Bert actually rubbed his big legs, sighed, and said, "Thanks...I've always wanted to do something like that, but never had the guts. And my ex-wife...well, she always wanted talking and romance. I'd ask her on the way home from a dinner party, I'd say, 'You wanna give me head right here in the car?'

and she'd say, 'Are you kidding...we can't do something like that...it's against the law.' All I can say is that when you get rejected enough, you develop an edge, and then you stop asking altogether."

Betty smiled and popped a breath mint into her mouth. "I don't know," she said, "I wish I were more like other women sometimes. But I really *don't* care about talking and romance and tons of psychological foreplay...I like sex; I like dick."

Bert leaned closer and laughed. "You want to know something else?" He began to whisper as if he were about to tell her his deepest darkest secret. "At first I was a little freaked out when I realized those two guys were watching you blow me, but then I realized I actually liked it. I mean I'm not gay or anything, but I sort of liked doing it in public. It felt dangerous and exciting."

She faced him and put her hands on her hips. "You knew all along?"

He nodded his head and said, "Sorry; I hope you're not mad or anything."

"Of course I'm not mad," she said. And then she hiked her skirt up and spread her legs a little. "If you like it so much, then why don't you take that little red toy out of my purse and do me now. We still have a very active audience, in case you haven't noticed."

Bert turned his head and looked over at the two guys across from him. The redhead was now going down on the dark-haired one. His head was bobbing up and down; the other guy's legs were stretched all the way out and his hand was in the middle of the redhead's shoulder blades. Bert looked at Betty and shrugged. "Open your legs wide, baby...and we won't need any toys for this, either." Then he waved his thick fingers and wagged his tongue.

WING WALKER

Cheyenne Blue

The conversations go something like this:

"I'm a wing walker," I say, demurely twiddling my glass of chardonnay.

"Oh?" he says, and his eyes flick over me dismissively, no doubt picturing me in thick overalls wielding an industrial hose of airplane deicer at DIA. "You don't look the maintenance type."

"I'm not," I say. "I wear a catsuit, not a boilersuit, and I dance on the wing of the plane as it flies along."

That always gets their attention, at the very least a double take, while they decide if I'm serious or not. And if they decide I am, then I have their interest for as long as I want it.

Wing walking goes something like this:

I dress warmly—a layer of wicking thermals because it's colder than the moon out there, with the wind whipping away every thought of warmth; then the catsuit. It's a patriotic red, white, and blue, a line of stars down the thigh, diagonal stripes over the torso. Patriotism goes down well with the air-show crowds. I wear goggles against the wind, soft slippers on my feet so I don't harm the fabric of the wing.

Bob is our pilot, Buttercup is our plane. Bob is sixty-eight and has a steady hand on the controls. Buttercup is also sixty-eight and she's a Boeing Stearman biplane, a game old girl painted as sunny as her name. Bob and her, they have a long history together. I often think they'll go together in a burst of flame on a hillside. I just hope I'm not on the wing at the time.

We take off from a back strip, away from the crowds. I'm already on the upper wing in my safety harness, securely fastened to the upright struts that protrude from the center of the plane's structure. Surely you didn't think I'd do this without a harness? Some people used to, but they tended to have short careers.

We circle the air show once, up high. We'll talk a little on the radio. Bob worries how long he can keep doing this. The maintenance on the old girl gets harder every year. Then we get the signal to go and we come in fast and low. I'll be in a pose: arm extended gracefully, my long hair streaming behind me like Boadicea the warrior queen. Or Xena the warrior princess—I guess more people have heard of her. One leg cocked up, I'll hold the pose and wave to the crowd as Bob takes us up in a hard spiral. And for the next fifteen minutes or so, Bob will twirl with Buttercup, looping the loop, flying upside down, flipping her from side to side, always within sight of the crowds, of course. And me? I'll be up there, posing, slow-motion dancing, sometimes doing a handstand, although Bob has to keep her totally steady for that one, so I only do that when he's been dry for a few days. The wind pummels the breath from my body, and moving a limb is like pushing against cement. The roar of the air and the rumble and creak of the plane beneath my feet fill my head. There's a crowd?

I honestly couldn't tell you. It's just me and Buttercup and Bob, flying in our little space-time continuum.

Evenings go something like this:

Me and Bob, in a Motel 6 somewhere, Buttercup in a hangar nearby. We get takeout and sit on one of the double beds, backs against the headboard, watching HBO. I trade some of my sweet and sour for Bob's lo mein, and we wrangle over who ate the most prawn crackers. We compromise on the wine: he likes sweet, I like dry, so as usual we settle on a Riesling, one of those big double bottles and we'll finish the lot.

"You need a man," Bob says, eyes on Sigourney Weaver, her singlet tastefully ripped as she battles aliens.

I grunt. "I can get one anytime I want."

"Not just a one-night man," says Bob. He knows about them. He's obligingly asked for another room on a few occasions when I can't go back to their place. "A real man."

"What man can compete with Buttercup?" I ask, adding hastily, "Apart from you."

"I'll find you a man," promises Bob. "One like Sigourney." So far, he hasn't.

Bob and I aren't lovers. There's a forty-year age gap. I like men with hair above the neck and none below. Bob likes men who are the reverse of that. We get along like old friends, sharing a room with two beds in each of the cheap motels to save money.

And so our evenings fill the space of a motel room and our mouths and hands follow the predictable routine of takeout and conversations we've had hundreds of times before. I wouldn't change those conversations; I wouldn't change Bob. Only the location of the Motel 6 changes. It teleports itself from Chino to Riverside to Prescott to Pueblo so that it's there when Bob and I fly up in Buttercup to prepare for the next show.

* * *

And one day, the conversation goes like this:

"Got you a man," says Bob, reaching over with a fork to snag a pork ball and dunk it in my sauce.

"Can get my own."

"Not that sort of man. Got you a man on the wing tomorrow."

Now my interest is up. Not many men wing walk. It's for the girls; the men are too chicken. Or too heavy. Can't have a two-hundred-pound man moving across the wing. Bob couldn't keep Buttercup steady if that happened.

"Name's Leon. He's a novice but he's keen. Thought we could try out some fancy-pants double act."

There's a mild alarm that I'll have to split my cut with this Leon, but I'm intrigued. I've never wing walked with a man, only girls, and there's always an element of competition in that. Whose tits can jut the farthest, whose leg can stay extended the longest, whose hair looks the best backswept and big as we leap lithely from the plane to greet the fans.

"Where'd you find him?"

"Came to the hangar when I was putting Buttercup to bed. We had a bit of a chat."

He must have been convincing. If I had a dollar for every person who says to me, "I did that once" or "I'd love to do what you do," I'd be rich enough to buy Bob his Mexican island staffed by Sigourney Weaver clones in loincloths. With dicks.

Leon is there the next morning. He's lean, feline like his name, small and wiry, the same height as me. He wears some sort of tight pants and a thick clinging fleece. The pants show off his ass pretty well. I think that he's probably gay. I'm wearing an old costume, stuff that is now not good enough for shows. There's a smear of oil across the chest and there's a couple of small holes:

one a rip on the thigh where I caught it on the door catch, the other a small one in the crotch where a seam gave when I did a handstand.

"Jaye, Leon, Leon, Jaye." Bob does the introductions and I check to see whether he's watching Leon's ass, but he's already turned away to fiddle with Buttercup's struts, so it's up to me and Leon to make conversation.

"When did you last do this?" I ask.

"Year or so ago."

"Where?"

He shrugs. "Mexico. Britain. Australia. Thailand."

Everywhere, it seems, but the States. Nowhere I'd have heard of him.

"Done it with another person before?"

He smiles, showing small white teeth. Both eyeteeth point in slightly; too poor for orthodontics. That's okay, so was my family. "Yeah. I don't like doing it alone."

Bob's finished fiddling and he produces a second harness. "You'll share the central brace," he says, "one on each side. Ain't had time to put up the other poles. We'll just take Buttercup up and see how you get along together up there."

I hoist up to the lower wing with ease; I do it all the time. When I stand up and look down, Leon's eyes whip away from my legs. He obviously likes women, at least a little.

We attach the harnesses firmly to the central pole, checking to make sure they won't tangle as we move around. It's a wide waist belt with shoulder straps and a slender steel cable that attaches to the pole. That's it: one skinny cable between me and eternity. My long hair is tightly braided and I wear a padded helmet as we're only practicing. No need for glamour this morning. The earpiece of the radio tucks into the side.

Bob turns the prop and Buttercup splutters into life. It's a crisp morning, and my hands are already tingling from the chill, but I don't like to wear gloves, I like to feel Buttercup beneath my palms. I see that Leon is bare-palmed, too—or maybe he doesn't have gloves. We trundle around to the runway, and Bob revs the engine. Normally, I'd brace myself against the back support as a lever against the wind as we take off—it's harder with two since we have to stand one on each side. But then we're up and the ground falls away beneath Buttercup's wings and the lift pushes my feet into the fabric.

Bob's voice comes over the radio. "I'll come around and level off at five hundred feet, and fly straight. Then you can do whatever it is you're going to do out there."

Beneath Buttercup's wings, there are cornfields and the yellow flat plains of eastern Colorado; a dry creek; a tangle of cottonwoods, yellowing in the early fall days; the huddle of hangars and huts around the airfield. Bob points her nose to the east and we fly into the slanting sun.

I grasp the support with one hand, lean out star fashion, tacitly encouraging Leon to do the same. He follows and when I glance left, he's arched into the wind, his face ecstatic. I shift to one foot, raise the other leg, point my toe, perform a slow series of poses around the pole. Leon follows a second behind. He's good at this.

"Going about," says Bob over the radio, and Leon nods, prepared to hold his pose through the bank and turn.

I'm the one watching him now, and there's a thrill in watching something so beautiful this close, watching some*one*, too. He's graceful; more deliberate in his movements than a woman, but no less glorious. With a thrill, I notice the hard lines of his thighs, the curve of his butt, the weight of his calves. And I notice, too, that in the wind, his suit is pulled tight across his groin, and he's erect. Not simply turgid from effort, but supporting a full-on pointing-to-the-right erection. Pointing to me. I glance again. He's not particularly long, but the outline looks thick. He must be really wound up for the cold and the wind not to send him as limp as one of Bob's lo mein noodles.

Two more passes of the airfield, and then Leon takes the lead. He handstands, as straight and steady as a redwood, his fingers splayed on the wing. He must be confident to try this so soon, with an unknown pilot and plane. Then his legs spread wide, and he holds the pose. Great abs. Another second, and his feet are lightly planted on the wing again.

He flashes me a smile, rests his butt against the pole, jack-knifes forward until he's in a cat stretch along the wing. I'm not trying to follow his moves. I'm simply watching him, his body, and trying to ignore the feelings in my cunt. It throbs in time with Buttercup's engine. The throb that tells me to radio Bob to get the hell down out of the sky, so that I can take Leon by the hand and find a quiet corner of the hangar to see if his dick is as delicious as it looks, flattened by his tight pants.

Leon stands. "You try," he mouths, the words whipped away by the wind.

Try what? I've been watching his body in the minutest detail, thinking of golden skin and muscles as hard as Buttercup's seat underneath that god-awful flying gear. I've been thinking of what he'll taste like, all sweat and adrenaline leaking out through his pores, and I haven't been paying attention to his moves.

He smiles. "Put your back against the support," he instructs, this time through the radio.

"Going around again," comes Bob's voice over the radio, and it's Leon who acknowledges him.

Leon waits until Buttercup steadies on her new course. Now we're heading west, toward the Rockies. I can see them, hazy and purple, tipped with caps of new snow.

He's behind me. His fingertips run along my body from shoulder to hip. "Good posture." His voice is tinny in my ear through the radio. It sounds strange with him being so close. "Try the cat stretch."

His hands remain at my waist as I jackknife. He's so close to me that I can feel the brush of his groin on my hip. He's still erect.

His hands travel slowly around the contours of my ass, one finger running over the crease of my pants. As bent over as I am, the gusset of my pants is biting into my pussy. The seam is pressing on my clit, and by clenching and releasing my ass, these tiny movements bring me higher. I must be red in the face from having my head so low, but I'm not straightening just yet. Beneath my feet, Buttercup flies on, and the rumble from her engine travels up my already heightened nerve pathways as the throbbing builds.

I can't hold the position forever, of course, so I arch out into his graceful cat stretch. His hands fall away from my ass, and the pressure eases between my legs, a temporary reprieve. I'm so horny I just want to bring myself back into reach of his hands.

I stand again, place my hip against the pole and wiggle my ass. As invitations go it's unsubtle, but we can't stay up here forever. Bob will be swinging Buttercup around any second and we'll be heading back to the airstrip. Leon rests against me and I feel the weight of his cock as he dry-humps himself, sliding over my shiny-suited ass. It's way too cold for him to unzip himself; he'd get frostbite in those delicate swollen tissues. Me, however…

His fingers work their way down the seam of my pants, and then, as I hoped, they find the hole. It's only a small one, an inch or so of torn seam, but it's right over my cunt. My hands tighten on the pole and my breathing is shallow. Buttercup trembles beneath my feet, Bob is humming to himself over the radio, the

Rockies are huge and purple and solid in my vision, and my cunt is fiery with need.

Leon slips two fingers into the hole. They brush lightly over my panties and I shudder. Then they scissor and the old thread gives way a little more, admitting three fingers. And now they brush rhythmically over the gusset. He must realize how wet I am. I grip the pole tightly with both hands and concentrate on his fingers, moving to and fro with deliberate intent.

"Heading back," says Bob over the radio, and there's a dip of Buttercup's wings as he prepares to turn.

Leon's hand twitches; I can sense his withdrawal. He's behind me, slightly stooped to work his fingers over my cunt. But he's also got his harness on and there's no danger. So I close my legs, trapping his hand. My inner thighs are tight and muscled from the wing walking, and he can't get away. He tries again, a tug, but his hand is trapped there as Buttercup banks around and heads back to the airfield.

Bob is still humming a Sousa march, and the sun is now hot on my face. Now that we've straightened out again, there's not long until we'll be on the ground. So I relax my thighs, free his hand, and Leon wiggles his fingers in appreciation. And then he starts to stroke in earnest, getting beneath my panties to caress my lips and circle my clit with an urgent fingertip.

I'm not sure if the ground is rushing up to meet me because Buttercup is coming in to land or if it's just the thrill and the buildup. But there's a tightness in my chest with the beauty and the glory of it all, and a trembling beneath my feet as Bob throttles back Buttercup's engine. And Leon's fingers are as fiery as the sun that burns my face and my world is tilting, the sky is falling or the ground is rising, and as Buttercup floats down out of the wide white sky, I come, screaming my joy into the wind.

Not a second too soon. Buttercup bumps down on the grass

and we're racing along, and Leon whips his hand away—I see his fingers shining with my juices—and we both grip the support tightly, totally unprepared for the landing.

Bob brakes and Buttercup meanders into her turn and taxis back to the hangar. I breathe slowly and deliberately, letting the world straighten itself again. I look over at Leon—my new partner—and smile, and he grins back with all the joy of flight in his eyes. The sun is golden on my face and Buttercup is steady beneath my feet. And here I am, on the wing, there with those that I love the most.

ABOUT THE AUTHORS

Written under the names Cheyenne Blue, Maggie Kinsella, and Charles LeDuc, **CHEYENNE BLUE**'s erotica has previously appeared in many anthologies, including previous volumes of *Mammoth Best New Erotica, Best Lesbian Romance, Best Women's Erotica,* three of the *Erotic Alphabet* series from Cleis Press, *Best Gay Romance*, and many other anthologies and websites from 2001 to the present. She has several stories upcoming in various anthologies.

ELIZABETH COLDWELL is the editor of the UK edition of *Forum* magazine. Her short stories have appeared in a number of anthologies including *Sex With Strangers, Best S/M Erotica 1* and *2, Yes, Sir* and *Spanked: Red Cheeked Erotica.* She believes that occasionally you have to make your own in-flight entertainment.

MATT CONKLIN is a dominant dirty old man who is even dirtier when he writes. He has penned many smutty tales on lonely, horny airplane rides. His writing has also been published in *Hide and Seek* and *He's on Top*.

DESIREE is a writer, foodie, and comic-book geek. She lives in Brooklyn, New York with her cat Ramses and has always had an inclination toward the naughty. She once scored seventy-six points in Scrabble with the word *clitoris*. She blogs about sex and life at www.baserinstincts.com, where she dares you to find any words misspelled.

JEREMY EDWARDS is a pseudonymous sort of fellow whose efforts at spinning libido into literature have been widely published online and have appeared in numerous print anthologies. His greatest goal in life is to be sexy and witty at the same moment—ideally in lighting that flatters his profile. Readers can drop in on him unannounced (and thereby catch him in his underwear) at http://jerotic.blogspot.com.

RYAN FIELD is a thirty-five-year-old freelance writer who lives and works in both Los Angeles, CA and New Hope, PA. His fiction has appeared in many erotic collections and anthologies. He is currently working on a novel that is based on some of his erotic experiences.

STAN KENT is a chameleon-hair-colored former nightclub-owning rocket scientist author of hot words and cool stories. A dedicated voyeur and world traveler, Stan has penned nine original, unique, and very naughty full-length novels including the *Shoe Leather* series and dozens of quickie reads on everything from spanking with shoes to cupcake sex to voyeuristic orgies to techno-rave group spankings on the dance floor. When not globe-trotting and jet-setting, Stan has hosted an erotic talk show night at Hustler Hollywood. The *Los Angeles Times* described his monthly performances as "combination moderator and lion tamer." To see samples of his works, his latest hair colors and travels, visit Stan at www.StanKent.com or email him at stan@stankent.com.

BILL KTE'PI is a full-time writer who has written fiction, encyclopedia entries, textbooks, academic essays, and assorted copy, while cultivating tastes beyond his means. He's currently on an extended layover in New England, and maintains a website at http://www.ktepi.com.

GENEVA KING (www.msgenevaking.com) has stories appearing in several anthologies including: *Ultimate Lesbian Erotica 2006, Best Women's Erotica 2006, Ultimate Undies, Caramel Flava*, and *Travelrotica for Lesbians 1 & 2*. A transplant to Northern Maryland, she's constantly on the prowl for her next muse.

ZACH LINDLEY was born in Sheffield, England, raised in Oregon and Nevada, but considers his home town to be Earth. He loves to examine the power of sensuality with the inimitable magic of the written word. He owes a debt of gratitude to his wife Magdalene, who is the breath of life to his erotica.

SOMMER MARSDEN's work has appeared in numerous online and print publications. Some of her favorites include: *I Is for Indecent; J Is for Jealousy; Yes, Sir; Love at First Sting; Ultimate Lesbian Erotica 2008; Forum UK;* Oysters and Chocolate; and Clean Sheets. To keep track of Sommer and her work (and her fat red wiener dog) go to http://SmutGirl.blogspot.com or visit her website www.freewebs.com/sommermarsden.

TERESA NOELLE ROBERTS has turned a perverted mind and insatiable curiosity about other people's sex lives into a career. Her short erotic fiction has appeared in dozens of anthologies, including *Spanked: Red-Cheeked Erotica; Yes, Sir: Erotic Stories of Female Submission; Yes, Ma'am: Erotic Stories of Male Submission; Lust: Erotic Fantasies for Women; Dirty Girls: Erotica for Women; Lipstick on Her Collar* and several volumes of *Best Women's Erotica.* She also writes as Sophie Mouette with coauthor Dayle A. Dermatis (Andrea Dale). Teresa loves to travel, but hates to fly.

THOMAS S. ROCHE's short stories have appeared in more than four hundred anthologies, magazines, and websites. He has written, edited or coedited more than ten books, including the *Noirotica* series of erotic crime-noir stories and the short-story collection *Dark Matter.* He also blogs about sex, drugs and cryptozoology and occasionally podcasts erotic fiction at www.thomasroche.com.

CRAIG J. SORENSEN has been flying the friendly skies since he was six months old. He has been crafting stories nearly as long. His erotic works have appeared online on Clean Sheets, Oysters and Chocolate, Lucrezia, and Ruthie's Club. He has had stories recently accepted for print anthologies.

DONNA GEORGE STOREY actually does love the smell of jet fuel on the breeze, morning, noon or night. Her erotica has appeared in many anthologies, including *Yes, Sir; He's on Top; She's on Top; Best Women's Erotica; The Mammoth Book of Best New Erotica* and *Best American Erotica 2006*. She is the author of *Amorous Woman* (Neon/Orion), the story of an American's love affair with Japan and her steamy encounters with many men and women along the way. Read more of her work at www.DonnaGeorgeStorey.com.

Called a "trollop with a laptop" by *East Bay Express* and a "literary siren" by Good Vibrations, **ALISON TYLER** is naughty and she knows it. Her sultry short stories have appeared in more than eighty anthologies including *Rubber Sex* (Cleis), *Dirty Girls* (Seal Press), and *Sex for America* (Harper Perennial). She is the author of more than twenty-five erotic novels, most recently *With or Without You* (Virgin), and the editor of more than forty-five explicit anthologies, including *J Is for Jealousy* (Cleis), *Naughty Fairy Tales from A to Z* (Plume), and *Naked Erotica* (Pretty Things Press). Please visit www.alisontyler.com for more information or http://www.myspace.com/alisontyler if you want to be her friend.

VANESSA VAUGHN is a twenty-something currently living in Dallas. After pursuing a short but successful career in nonprofit fundraising, she is now devoting herself to what she loves best: writing. Some of the many things that turn her on include vampires, tennis skirts, long cigarettes, any woman from a Wachowski Brothers movie, tattoos, uni, gold bullion, Stephen Colbert, WOW geeks, burlesque, and fine wine, in no particular order. This is her first published work.

In high school, **KRISTINA WRIGHT** was known as the girl most likely to be a writer—but no one could have predicted what this former "good girl" would end up writing. Kristina's fiction has appeared in over fifty anthologies, including *Best Women's Erotica, The Mammoth Book of Best New Erotica*, and *Bedding Down: Winter Erotica*. She loves to travel, but she's never run into an old boyfriend...yet. For more information about Kristina, visit her website, www.kristinawright.com.

ABOUT THE EDITOR

RACHEL KRAMER BUSSEL (www.rachelkramerbussel.com) is an author, editor, blogger, and reading series host. She has edited or coedited over twenty books of erotica, including *Do Not Disturb: Hotel Sex Stories; Tasting Him; Tasting Her; Spanked: Red-Cheeked Erotica; Naughty Spanking Stories 1* and *2; Yes, Sir; Yes, Ma'am; He's on Top; She's on Top; Caught Looking; Hide and Seek; Crossdressing; Rubber Sex; Sex and Candy; Ultimate Undies; Glamour Girls; Bedding Down* and the nonfiction collections *Best Sex Writing 2008* and *2009*. Her work has been published in over one hundred anthologies, including *Best American Erotica 2004* and *2006*, Zane's *Chocolate Flava 2* and *Purple Panties, Everything You Know About Sex is Wrong, Single State of the Union* and *Desire: Women Write About Wanting*. She serves as senior editor at *Penthouse Variations*, and wrote the popular "Lusty Lady" column for the *Village Voice*.

Rachel has written for *AVN, Bust*, Cleansheets.com, *Cosmopolitan, Curve*, Fresh Yarn, The Frisky, Gothamist, Huffington

Post, Mediabistro, *Newsday, New York Post, Penthouse, Playgirl, Radar, San Francisco Chronicle, Tango, Time Out New York*, and *Zink,* among others. She has been quoted in the *New York Times, USA Today, Maxim UK, Glamour UK, GQ Italy, National Post* (Canada), *Wysokie Obcasy* (Poland), *Seattle Weekly,* and other publications, and has appeared on "The Martha Stewart Show," "The Berman and Berman Show," NY1, and Showtime's "Family Business." She has hosted In The Flesh Erotic Reading Series since October 2005, about which the *New York Times*'s UrbanEye newsletter said she "welcomes eroticism of all stripes, spots and textures." She blogs at lustylady.blogspot.com and cupcakestakethecake.blogspot.com.